The Rag Doll Plagues

Alejandro Morales

Arte Publico Press
Houston
Texas
1992

Acknowledgements

This volume is made possible by a grant from the National
Endowment for the Arts, a federal agency.

Arte Publico Press
University of Houston
Houston, Texas 77204-2090

Cover design and Illustration by Mark Piñón

Morales, Alejandro, 1944–
   The rag doll plagues: a novel / by Alejandro Morales.
         p.   cm.
   ISBN 1-55885-036-8
   I. Title.
PS3563.O759R34 1991
863–dc20   91-2381
                                                CIP

The paper used in this publication meets the minimum requirements of the American National
Standard for Permanence of Paper for Printed Library Materials Z39.48-1984. ∞

The Rag Doll Plagues, a creation of fiction and poetry, is a work of history and the imagination. Any truth or similarity between characters and people, living or dead, is unexpected.

Thanks to

Jo-Ann Mapson, John French

John Jay Tepaske, David Margileth

UC MEXUS

This book is dedicated to

my children Gregory Stewart and Alessandra Pilar

imagination and inspiration from the genesis

The Rag Doll Plagues

Book One

MEXICO CITY

1

Delicate features distinguished the brown faces of the carved angels sounding trumpets from the opulent baroque doorway of the royal palace in the City of Mexico. Don Juan Vicente de Guemes Pacheco de Padilla, count of Revilla Gigedo, gentleman of the Royal Bed-Chamber, Knight of the Holy Order of Alcántara, Captain of the Regal Guard and Viceroy of New Spain, resided here with his wife, Doña María Alfonsina de Toledo and their two daughters. The cherub's golden wings shimmered in the afternoon sun, which passed over the center of the Main Plaza, and contrasted with the filthy central fountain where Indians, Mestizos, Negroes, Mulattoes and the other immoral racial mixtures of humanity drank and filled clay jugs with foul dark water while they socialized. In 1788, I, a loyal physician and surgeon to his Majesty the King of Spain, rode in an elegant viceregal carriage, bearing the Viceroy's escutcheon. It had been sent to Veracruz by my longtime friend, the Count of Revilla Gigedo. He had dispatched the carriage so that I might travel in comfort and splendor to the seat of power, the capital of New Spain and the heart of his world—a world I had at first refused to visit. But because the King ordered my presence to help our mutual friend, the Viceroy, I have come to endure the filth and corruption of this demoralized capital.

The perils of the journey from the Gulf to the City of Mexico were not diminished by traveling in such a grand carriage. In fact, the journey became more dangerous, perhaps not for me, but for the Indian *tamemes*—professional carriers—who crossed over their foreheads wide leather straps to help support the massive loads they carried. Long ropes were attached to the head straps, to which were

11

tied my *petacas*, heavy leather trunks with medical instruments, medicine and my personal estate. They lugged the *petacas* on their backs. These Indians were bald and scarred. Their foreheads were calloused and deformed from a lifetime of service. I was fascinated by the strength and durability of their emaciated bodies. They kept moving for as long as I advanced. They appeared cool and concentrated, as if in a trance.

At about mid-day, an Indian scout reported that the bridge over the river had been washed away. Our mestizo escort spoke to the carriers, and shortly afterward we took a secondary road, which led to the narrowest part of the river where the strong current was only chest high. The Indians first crossed with the trunks, then, although I resisted, they made me sit in a chair mounted on the back of the tallest and strongest man, who proceeded to carry me across. Four Indians walked alongside him for support, in case he misjudged the treacherously smooth rocks. Extending my arms, I defied the Indians touching me; still, they held my feet above the water so that I would not get wet. Safely across, I rested on a sculptured oak chair and observed the preparations for the crossing of the carriage. Four long wooden poles locked the wheels in place and allowed the Indians to lift the carriage above their shoulders. Eight bearers stepped carefully up to their waist into the steady current while other Indians moved along ready to take over in case of any mishaps. Suddenly, before entering the water, one collapsed below the left rear wheel and caused his partner to give under the weight. For a minute, the full weight of the carriage rested on the Indian's chest, then the wheel slowly rolled and crushed his throat, face and head. The first Indian, who had collapsed, disappeared into the river. I stood and moved closer to the water's edge, from where I heard the popping sounds of the dead Indian as he was pulled away from the sucking mud. The guide hurried the carriers along and the carriage began to ford the river. Nearby, two Indians deposited their dead brother into the muddy water, bound by his own ropes to two pieces of driftwood. The body floated down river and came to a stop amongst hundreds of skulls and bones lying in whitening heaps along the river bank.

I was determined to show no fear to these savages who could not possibly have souls. For a long distance the road followed the river. I glimpsed out to see fully clothed corpses being lapped by the current. The river was treacherous, but not to this appalling extent. In one instance, I beheld numerous cadavers in different stages of decay trapped on a sharp river bend. I pondered the cause of these deaths. Don Juan Vicente's letters described a disease that had killed hundreds, but that had left as quickly as it had materialized. Were these unfortunate remains the aftermath of the malady?

Poverty and illness attracted me, as if I needed to get closer to that which I rejected. On the way to Mexico City I had experienced this emotion once before. The intense colors of the flowers and plants, the beautiful birds and the massive trees and vines of the extraordinary rain forest were the jungle I had read about and imagined. As my caravan went along, young natives reached out with open palms and ran alongside the carriage.

We stopped at a bamboo thatched inn. The innkeeper offered various plates and drinks from which I chose a meal of fish and fruit, and I drank a special Rioja which Don Juan Vicente had sent with the carriage. Although some of the clients were foul-smelling, I found no person, man or woman, offensive. People kept their distance. They ate, drank, danced and sang along with a trio of Indian musicians: a harpist, two mandolin players. In a corner, a woman sold a kind of white liquor, while two others sat on their calves and, with a stone roller and table, ground corn and shaped round flat bread into tortillas. With each downward stroke of the stone rolling pin, the older woman's breasts swayed freely into my sight, absorbing me into a sexual reverie. But, how could any man sin with these soulless creatures of God?

A drunken man abruptly interrupted my daydreams and spoke of an Amazon woman with ample breasts of warmth and love. She was reputedly the territory's best and most famous muleteer, despite being a woman. The man rambled on about how this woman, known as La Monja Alférez, had rebelled against the authorities of her convent and had run away in male attire. She had made her way from Spain to the New World not only dressed as a man but able to handle a sword as well. In a few years, she became the terror of the road from Mexico City to Veracruz. According to the man, La Monja Alférez had taken many lives. Her dueling and killing had brought her into conflict with the authorities, who pursued her until finally she was captured and sentenced to hang. But she was spared her life when she revealed to the Royal Courts that she was a woman, a nun and a virgin. The latter she proved by exposing a chastity belt that she had worn since her first menstruation. The royal courts found her to be so bizarre that they sent her to Spain to have an audience with the King and the Pope. The King gave her a pension for life and the Pope a dispensation to wear male clothing for the rest of her remaining time on earth. She returned to Mexico, where she developed a thriving mule skinning business. Her life came to a climax when she fell in love with the smell, taste, touch and voice of another woman. Her lover was the Spanish wife of a young *hidalgo* who discovered them in succulent copulations. The enraged husband forced La Monja Alférez naked into the street. Hours later, La Monja Alférez returned to challenge the devastated man to a mortal duel. He did not hesitate to answer and in his haste he committed only one fatal movement, which allowed La Monja Alférez to skewer the *macho* from his screaming mouth through his bleeding anus. As the good gentleman lay dying, she embraced her lover and rode off with her on an effulgent black mule. Charges were never brought against La Monja Alférez, and to this day she lived with her Spanish female lover and their ebony mule.

Laughter filled the tavern. The man extended his open palm. But the owner only pushed the drunken man out the door. I thought he had spoken for a long while, but his story had really taken only a matter of minutes.

Fear extends time.

For the killing of the young *hidalgo*, I would have made an example of the witch by burning her at the stake.

With the unbearable loud pounding of horse's hooves on the stones of the main causeway, I arrived into the city. The coachman identified the buildings along the way and slowed down so that I might partake of their architectural beauty, but to me, the decadence of the city was evident everywhere.

I sat back comfortably in the silk seat of the expensive carriage and wondered how the magnificence of the buildings, the wide avenues and the parks had been allowed to fall into such disarray and indecency. Even the well-dressed men and women of obvious Spanish upbringing and education walked slowly with the pallor of illness upon their countenance. The peasants and the slaves ambled in ragged, grimy clothing, their feet heavily wrapped in rags. The lepers moved in groups avoiding contact with the other profligates of the city.

"The university!" the coachman called out. The university where I had ordered the cooperation of my physicians. For their own good, they would assist me in what needed to be done to improve the state of medicine here in the colonies. For years the university, the theologians, the canon and civil lawyers, the doctors of Scripture, Rhetoric, Logic and Metaphysics had held the medical profession in low esteem. There was no more tainted blood and the examinations and certification procedures had been improved. I had come to the New World to implement these new procedures. As First Professor of Medicine, Anatomy and Surgery in His Majesty's Empire, as First Physician and Surgeon of the Royal Bedchamber and as the Director of the Royal *Protomedicato*, I had worked to improve the medical profession. Despite being the youngest director ever appointed by the King and approved by my colleagues throughout the Empire, I had faced resistance to change and especially to the new institute of medical research that I had established in Spain and here at the university. This institute would implement the latest medical advancements of Europe and apply them here to the native population. The physicians in Mexico would begin to study these new discoveries and make them available to the mass population. In this way, the male and female Spanish-speaking practitioners of witchcraft, the popular *curanderos*, would be forced out of circulation. These *curanderos* were dangerous and had caused the deaths of thousands. Worst of all were the Indian *curanderos* who practiced witchcraft in their native tongue. They had to be prevented from practicing their evil craft.

As the director of the *Protomedicato*, I came to assess the medical needs of His Majesty's colonies. By improving the health and medical treatment of the common population, the King desired to avoid a spirit of separatism here. He was well aware that the French revolutionary emotion was contagious and that the success of the United States independence movement could effect the future direction of the Empire. The people of the colonies had to be convinced that they were better off living as part of the Empire than separate from it. Therefore I was here to quell the fires of revolutionary fervor by extinguishing the illnesses in the fevered populace.

"The Convent of San Jerónimo!"

The carriage stopped in a clean refreshing garden opposite a convent.

"Your Royal Apartments, sir!"

2

I stood before the entry of my residence and contemplated the lovely, fine-sculptured flowers, fruits and classical male and female figures cheering my presence. Their dark Indian faces smiled and watched with almond-shaped eyes my every gesture as I moved into the exquisite foyer which lead into a large luxurious reception hall. On the walls, grand portraits of past viceroys stared down from massive golden, ornate frames. Above them, austere archbishops and cardinals offered a silent blessing. Standing on stone shelves overhead, pure white marble statues of the holy apostles pointed to the heavens. As I studied the hall, the Indian servants carried trunks to my quarters. I waited in silence. I was captivated by the wonders created by these primitive people. For almost three hundred years we attempted to bring these Indians out of their ignorance. We gave them a soul, but some still spurned the grace of God and remained heathen. We had to take better care of them, for God had consigned them to us. If we neglected this charge, then the Empire would crumble. In these artistic creations were the manifestations of God's light deep within their pagan existence. To guarantee our survival we had to make that light shine.

I wandered out to a peaceful garden, where frenzied hues of roses were guarded by statues of the apostles Mark, Luke, John and Matthew, each at respective corners, holding their versions of the Gospel. In gardens as beautiful as these, my betrothed, Renata, and I had walked and discussed biblical events and people. We had discussed our marriage. We had planned to live in Madrid close to her parents' estate.

Her father had resisted our engagement for several years. Finally, after my appointment as director, he agreed to consider the marriage of his daughter to a doctor. Renata was ecstatic when she related her father's decision to me in the garden of their home. The colors of the flowers became brighter, their aroma exhilarating, the air sweeter, the sky a clearer blue on that spring afternoon. No more obstacles stood before us. We could not hold back our desire for one another and we embraced. Her father coughed. Her mother nudged Renata's lady in waiting toward her. Suddenly from the rooms adjacent the garden, applause broke out and Renata's three sisters and three brothers and their families ran out to celebrate our joy.

Later that evening, I discovered that for months, the family had lobbied Renata's father to give his blessing to our union and to make an official announcement of the marriage banns.

Six months later, I was summoned by the King and ordered to the colonies to aid the Viceroy. Renata waited for me. Perhaps from her garden at home she sent prayers and kisses.

I could not guess at the number of times I had passed-by each authorial apostle. Perhaps the altitude of Mexico City had begun to effect my strength and perception. I felt drowsy among the redolent flowers. My legs were weak and my feet attempted to feel the stone path. Why had I been left alone? Don Juan Vicente promised that an assistant would be at my side always! Why was there nobody here?

With cupped hands I scooped the crystal clear water of the fountain and refreshed my face, neck and arms. From the tone of the trickling water there emerged a presence of someone other than myself in that garden of peace. I searched the pathways in front, to the right and to the left of me. Fear and great vulnerability suddenly came upon me. I sensed that someone had silently and powerfully taken over the space directly behind me.

"Before you turn to face me," a voice said, "be forewarned. Be not shocked at what you are about to regard."

What could surpass the decadence and death that I had seen thus far on my voyage to the heart of the New World? Oh God, what were you about to test me with now? My question was a prayer as I turned and faced the mask of death itself. It stood only ten feet away.

A living skull, a monk from whose face the nose and upper lip had been sliced away to reveal long, deep, opened nostrils and upper gums and teeth. I forced my eyes to see this man who stood proudly before me as he moved closer. I held my ground. I did not falter.

"Allay your dread. I am of this world. The Viceroy has sent me to assist you in your institutional obligations. My name is Father Jude and my face is the test given to me by our Lord through the violence of renegade French pirates of the Caribbean. The Viceroy hopes you will agree to my service." Father Jude waited.

In that pause, I glanced at the flowers and settled my mind to think of the appropriate response to this maimed priest. The wind stirred and a stench gradually permeated the garden of perfume. The foulness did not come from him. It invaded from the outside, from that strange world out there. I responded not out of pity, but to Don Juan Vicente's wish to have this priest facilitate my work here. Don Juan Vicente, a man of wise council whom I would not contradict. I noticed a smile form on the lower lip of my attendant.

"In time you will become accustomed to my countenance," Father Jude said apologetically.

"What is that putrid smell?" I asked.

"Probably the dead and the dying, Don Gregorio." Father Jude crossed himself and raised his eyes to the heavens.

I saw the red moist flesh of his inner nostrils.

3

Several elegantly decorated rooms constituted my quarters. Fine silks, linens and furs doused with wonderful perfumes enhanced my bedchamber. Flowers had been placed on every table, but still the stench of suffering persisted amongst the rich bouquets.

After dinner, Father Jude led me to a library adjacent to my rooms. There we sat, the grotesquely lacerated priest and me, the powerless man of medicine. His impairments reminded me of my limitations as a doctor. If I could only place my hands on him and make him whole, I would have. He poured brandy and smiled. He placed the glass against his lower teeth and slowly tilted his head back. His exposed upper gums and teeth were hideous to me still, but I would not show my repulsion.

I relaxed in the thought of my friend Don Juan Vicente. "I want to see the Viceroy tomorrow morning, at the Royal Palace."

"The Viceroy is at his residence outside of the city," Father Jude answered.

"The Viceroy does not reside at the Royal Palace?"

"The palace is in disrepair. During the day, some administrative business is transacted there, but at night the diseased sleep in its corridors. The Viceroy has ordered it renovated," Father Jude said and took a deep breath through his naked nasal cavities.

The reasons for this decadence and corruption escaped me. Had not our administrators been concerned with the welfare of the Empire? Had not King Charles III's policies improved the condition of life? Had not his predecessor, his Majesty, Charles IV, continued them? Surely the Viceroy was dedicated to his subjects here. Was

I not sent here to improve the medical profession by orders of his Majesty himself?

"Father Jude, why am I here?" I asked, already anticipating his initial response. "Why am I really here?"

"We are grateful that you are here. We believe that you will be able to help us change the public health facilities and the general practice of physicians. Yes, you must complete your duties as the Director of the *Protomedicato*. But more urgent than this is a challenge that you must confront almost immediately. It is a matter of life and death for thousands, perhaps even millions," Father Jude said, his voice solemn. He poured more brandy.

"A great plague has erupted and poisoned our populace. It has ravaged the country and it is now moving into the capital. We have applied all medical knowledge in vain. The monster spreads and horribly kills our people. It first attacked the Indians and now it infects the Spaniards. This disease takes everyone, regardless of sex, race, age or rank. It is a just disease," Father Jude said and sipped his brandy.

"What do you mean 'just'?" I was astounded and angered by his statement.

"I mean this disease does not exclusively kill Indians, like the many European plagues your people brought to the New World. You and your kind are not immune. If infected, you will die. What we face is an unknown plague. Perhaps it is one of those that several times throughout history has destroyed the great Indian cultures here. I am ignorant of the origin of the cursed contamination. I am afraid that if we fail to arrest it, all of Mexico will be depopulated and the Empire exterminated." Father Jude spoke with fervor.

It was as if the extermination of the Empire brought joy to him. He suddenly raised a scarf to his nostrils and grotesquely discharged what sounded like congested mucus. He regained his composure.

"The bodies on the river?" I asked.

He nodded. "Victims of floods and now of plague. In less than three months the disease has killed thousands."

"I am sure we have dealt with this illness before," I said confidently.

"Never. It begins like the pox, but only on the extremities of the body. Then in a few days, it does horrendous damage to the internals. The suffering is great then, but when it gets to the trunk and head, it is indescribable. I can take you to a hospital tomorrow. You will see for yourself. If you want to go. You are aware of the dangers." He delighted in his challenge to me.

"Are you not afraid for you life?" I asked defensively.

"Even though I live with this great mutilation, you mean? I love life. I am the only person who will treat these people." Father Jude walked to the door.

"You are a doctor?"

"No, but I know medicine. Do you wish to come tomorrow?" Father Jude waited. I could hear his breathing.

"Yes, I must do my work!" I answered as if I had to eradicate any doubts that Father Jude might have as to my commitment to help the sick.

"At dawn then." Father Jude paused for a moment. "Please forgive my boldness, but I must comply with the Viceroy's request that I see to your every need, for if I do not, he will surely lose his confidence in me. Thus, I must ask you, Don Gregorio, if you are desirous of sexual alleviation. I have at my disposal delightful virgins, male and female, that are prepared to bend to your every pleasure." Embarrassed but amused, Father Jude bowed his ugly head.

"No." I answered curtly.

Father Jude bowed at the waist, took three steps back, turned and was gone.

I found myself forlorn and secluded at the center of a sick world.

4

That night my sleep was restless. I closed my eyes, slept for an hour at the most and was awakened by a sigh, a murmur, a word coming from without and within the walls of my room. The sound of footsteps woke me again. I sat up, looking in the corners for the individual who only moments earlier I had heard walk by the foot of the bed. Finally I lay down, determined not to get up. I needed to rest, to sleep, if only for a few hours. With sleep came a vision. I stood outside a small adobe room watching two men move toward me. They talked freely, laughed and seemed to enjoy each others' company. Their dress was so different from mine that I searched for my clothes to compare. I found them lying on a sofa in the middle of a grass field. I dressed and noticed that there were strange wires overhead running from pole to pole. A large blue and white carriage parked beyond a fence moved without horses. The strangeness of the place became wondrous. Heading toward the horizon, two large birds flew slowly above. I noticed that the men were almost upon me. One was a man in his fifties, perhaps even older. His face was marked with experience. The other was a young fellow, about eighteen to twenty years. I was not afraid. It was as if I knew these men. The young man reached out to shake my hand. "Gregorio," my own name was repeated countless times. Enormous monoliths of time, places and people circulated among us, always preventing us from consummating our handshake. With the old man leading, we traveled together. Gregorio and I moved as one in the same person, viewing the world from within each other. We were astonished with the marvels of our worlds, amazed at the facility of stepping through one another into another time, place, situation and the people we loved. Voices multiplied and more voices appeared from throughout time. I recognized all but one—my own.

Confused, I turned to Gregorio for direction and saw him looking to me for help. From a great distance, the old man floated toward and away from us. Impossibility composed normality. He proceeded through a multitude of transformations, as did Gregorio and I, one step behind. Our potential was profound. Unprecedented power was at our hands. No obstacles deterred our exploration.

While a serpent coiled around Gregorio's body, a man and a woman prayed in my room to the *Virgen de Guadalupe*. Voices screamed and I understood from both sides of my brain. A light appeared and from it alighted the old man to point the way to the path we were to follow.

"Papá Damián, you have come to be our guide."

He smiled and said in a throng of voices, "I will return you to your houses."

I lay in bed, my eyes opened, waiting for the New World sun. At dawn someone knocked at my door, waited for me to answer and left. Shortly after breakfast, Father Jude arrived with the carriage and an escort of eleven heavily armed royal guardsmen. Two extra horses rode with the caravan. Father Jude's horse, a black imposing animal of well over eighteen hands, was followed by a grey Arabian, proudly high-stepping alongside the carriage. After food, drink, my medical bag and supplies were loaded on a cart, we were on our way to the Hospital de los Santos Mártires, situated south of the city. We traveled on the Calzada de Traspana, one of the six main entrances to the New World's largest city, which measured three miles East to West and four miles from North to South. It was built on top of the destroyed Aztec city of Tenochtitlan in the middle of Lake Texcoco by Indian and Mestizo slave labor directed by Spanish architects. As we moved deeper into the bowels of the city, I found that the living conditions could only be described as stomach-wrenching. Upon my entering the city for the first time I had observed horrible sanitary conditions in the Central Plaza, but those seemed trite compared to what I was seeing now. Only a block from my residence I was shocked by the bodies of hundreds of dead dogs in a pile covered with a blanket of flies that undulated like a black hair net on and above the decaying carcasses. Utterly filthy people argued over the freshest ones.

Father Jude pointed to a portico with four columns and crossing arches crowned by an ominous iron cross with a sword and an olive branch at its base.

Father Jude entwined his fingers and bowed his head. "Symbols of mercy."

I sensed irony in his statement. In his pious posture there was an attitude of mockery towards the Holy Office of the Inquisition. Inside that palace of stone mazes, of secret passageways, cells and torture chambers of atonement, lived the three Inquisitors and other ministers of the Holy Office.

As we passed the Palace of the Inquisition, men and women squatted facing each other and deposited excrement and urine into the canal that ran down the center of the street. As they met their human needs, they conversed with ease and cordiality. Upon finishing, they simply raised their garment and walked away. They had no paper nor cloth to practice anal hygiene. It was cleaner to defecate and stand than to employ your hand to wipe away the clinging or watery excess. Nonetheless, many adults and children did use their hands. The windows of the houses along this street were tightly closed in a desperate attempt to keep out the gases of decaying animal and human waste.

Immediately before the carriage, a window suddenly opened. Without warning, a pail of excrement and urine was tossed out. At many points, the drainage ditch running down the middle of the street was clogged with the manure and urine from animals and human beings. Puddles formed in which to my absolute consternation I observed children playing happily. When a cart would roll through the puddles, its wheels stirred up an intolerable rankness.

I had noticed that Father Jude always covered his face with a black veil; now I saw it was not because of his mutilation, but for the filthy stench of the city. I finally believed what I was seeing. This was not a nightmare, but His Majesty's Empire. The carriage moved about a block further south and still people squatted along the drainage canal tending to their daily necessities. We stopped abruptly to find that our path had been blocked by a brown, putrid ooze emerging from the soft bottom of Lake Texcoco. The cobblestone street, pounded for decades by carriages, had cracked severely, allowing the pestilential muck to rise to the surface.

We retreated to work our way around the brown thick lava-like filth that spread with every minute.

Quickly, the driver avoided the deepest part by skirting to the outside and away from the rising slime. Again, the carriage came to a sudden halt, but this time it was before a crowd of desperate wailing people whose feet were heavily wrapped in rags and paper.

A young woman seemed to be aimlessly meandering through the street, carrying the body of a dead girl. No doubt it was her daughter, struck down by the disease. Following her, there came two cartmen who had the responsibility of disposing of the dead. The woman refused to give up her child. She saw our carriage. She ran toward it and threw her child at the window. I saw the child's limp naked body directly below. Her arms and legs were like stockings of skin, grotesquely swollen, reddish blood as is sausage.

"The Last Rites for my child!" the woman screamed. "Mercy for the poor!" several people cried out.

Only the woman's moan interrupted the silence of the void that death had created. Father Jude descended from the carriage, went to the girl's mother, blessed her and recited prayers for the dead and the innocent. With the holy words spoken and the mother calmed, the cartmen took the child and placed her on top of a pile of dead. The woman followed behind, sobbing. Father Jude observed the people heading to the pauper's grave. I had seen the woman's eyes and I felt cursed.

As if invisible to all but me, I noticed Papá Damián and Gregorio, who hurried to catch up to the burial procession. The people appeared to take no notice of their odd attire.

From the Main Plaza, the residential areas were organized around churches, which towered over the homes of the common population. There were about twenty-one churches of varied sizes and ornamentation in the city. Every zone had its special plaza, fountain and church where religious and secular celebrations were observed. Second to the last zone in the south was located the infamous bordello section. This section was the culmination of disgrace and filth. Father Jude stopped there to minister to dying male and female prostitutes who suffered from the epidemic and/or venereal diseases.

As we approached a small chapel where the moribund waited for Father Jude, I saw a scantily garbed woman performing fellatio at the entrance to one of the bordellos. These manifestations of the devil demonstrated no shame or inhibition whatsoever. She performed more vigorously. The man's body became rigid and, with his eyes shut, allowed this lewd act to reach its culmination. The clientele of the different houses nonchalantly stopped and observed for a moment, laughed, made some ribald remark and entered the whore house.

Inside the chapel, the only sacred and respected place in the area, while Father Jude prayed for the sick, I made my way to the fountain where a young man sodomized a boy as others waited their turns. All around the square, men, women and children negotiated a price for their hedonistic carnal acts.

After terminating their lustful deeds, a few men, women and children cleansed their genitalia with the murky water. A short distance away, the murmur of prayer came from the chapel of the prostitutes. For a moment, peace reigned over this city of debauchery. Several women approached, exposed their breast and lifted their dresses to show me their genitalia. They walked away angry and cursing my restraint. Children demonstrated how they would masturbate me. Some opened their mouths and knelt before me.

An old hag ran from the chapel of the prostitutes screaming, "Ay! She's dead! Another one of God's whores is dead!"

Is there no way out of this sinful state of life, I thought, as Father Jude prayed over the body of a young woman who had been taken out of the chapel and laid on the ground to wait for the cemetery cart.

"That woman's mouth and head were horribly distorted," I said as we road to the hospital.

"She was a mere child of twelve, insane and deformed by syphilis. Just another one of the millions who have benefited from our Majesty's policies," Father Jude snorted. "I am the only person who treats them. I help them die."

He removed the veil from his face, wiped his chin and carefully cleaned his exposed nasal orifices. His lacerations were nothing compared to the physical and mental wounds of the people to whom he ministered. His flock was a diseased, infested population: the prostitutes, the lepers, the abandoned children, the demented homeless people, the disenfranchised who survived in the filthy streets, the dungheaps and the garbage dumps of the city. Along with the laboring enslaved poor, these were Father Jude's patients, who looked to him not only for physical and spiritual remedies, but for an insurgent attitude that made life tolerable and nurtured a growing desire for change. Father Jude veiled his face again, leaned his head back on the carriage's cushioned head-rests, breathed deeply and for a moment seemed to relax.

Where the aqueduct turned away from the stones of the Calzada de Traspana, barely outside of the city, the road became dirt. Directly in our path there rose a block prison-like structure, with turrets on its four corners. Three large chimneys bellowed smoke and a large crucifix hung over the tall main entrance. Our entourage halted beside several women dressed in burlap togas who were sweeping, circling monotonously over the same area of the entrance patio of the Hospital de los Santos Mártires.

As Father Jude handed me my medical bag, he explained, "This church was converted by the Jesuits into a hospital for demented women. After they left, it became a hospital for people afflicted with acute or unexplainable diseases. The women patients remained."

No sounds were heard outside the thick walls of the hospital, but as we entered, the cries and moans were unbearable. I was a doctor. I remained as calm as the angel of mercy who had brought me here. In the central patio, two nuns waited. Each one wore a thin red silk ribbon on the collar of her black habits. For our protection,

they offered large padded cloth boots to cover our shoes. Father
Jude refused. I did likewise. The nuns expressed obvious joy at our
presence. They repeatedly crossed themselves and bowed toward
me in a posture of prayerful thanksgiving. Amidst the cries of the
ailing, their silent thanks reverberated. How strange that all of
our communication was done in silence. The youngest of the two
sisters had beautiful blue eyes and with them she indicated the path
to follow.

Father Jude spoke as we walked behind the two nuns. "You
will visit three wards. In the first are the patients with the initial
symptoms of *La Mona*, the name that the people have given this
disease. For when life withdraws from the body, *La Monita* leaves
a corpse that feels like a rag doll. The body never hardens, as in a
natural death, but remains soft like a wineskin. In the second ward,
you will see the patients in the secondary stages of the disease. In
the third ward are the dying, those who will probably not make it
through the day. In this last ward, the disease has damaged primarily
the head and the brain. Patients in this last state are unpredictable."

All along the cold white corridor, demented women roamed
aimlessly, mumbling, screaming naked on the ground. Some sat
in their excrement. Some slept while others pulled at their hair or
ripped away at their clothes, and many others, I am sure, simply
lay dead. No one was there to help. The two sisters stopped before
the first ward and motioned for me to proceed. Their faces emitted
joy. Living in this hospital of madness and death, there seemed
to be neither any desperation nor sadness in them that I detected.
Ignorant of what humanity should feel when confronted with such
calamity, I turned to the hideous Father Jude, who motioned for me
to come forward.

In what used to be a dormitory ward, hundreds of infected people of all ages sat or slept on the floor. Their feet were thickly bound
with layers of rags as to form large round cloth balls which made
them waddle when they walked. These people were the initiates of
La Mona.

"You see the illness begins by attacking the extremities of the body. The feet or the hands are usually the first members to be affected," Father Jude said and motioned to a man and a woman to unravel the ball of rags on their feet.

"Their toes are swollen, in three to five days they will turn reddish, and soon after the bones and muscles will dissolve into a pus-like ooze," Father Jude whispered. He examined the woman. "She is far more advanced into *La Mona*. Her feet are leather bags of pus. She probably is unable to walk," Father Jude said.

Four children carrying water stood by the couple. There was no need to ask to whom they belonged.

"This couple came here in hopes that after their death their children will be cared for. But usually the poor souls never leave. They stay and care for their dying parents and soon after they join them. Look at the reddish hue on this child's hands." Father Jude sighed through his black veil.

The decaying humanity cried out to the priest and me as we made our way about the ward. Finally we arrived at the second ward, from which a greater stench emitted. Smiling, the sisters slowly opened the two heavy doors.

Most of the patients in this ward lay moaning or screaming. The disease had consumed at least one limb completely and had begun to attack the torso. Some had one of their arms like an inflated goat intestine through which *La Mona* climbed and gnawed at their shoulders or necks. To others, *La Mona* liquified the hip and passed on to the lower intestine.

"If the illness moves on the neck it can either move vertically or horizontally. If it travels upward, it eventually consumes the face and brain. If it moves sideways, it either strangles or drowns the victim," Father Jude explained, pointing to several patients.

As we moved on, I noticed people with open wounds on their arms or legs, expelling a pasty putrid pus. I observed a man with a knife as he slit his leg from the knee down to his foot. The leg tissue offered no resistance. The man and I watched a substance slowly pour out from his body.

"Did he feel pain?" I asked Father Jude, who had motioned to one of the sisters to clean the man's spillings.

"The pain is concentrated where the disease is eating away and digesting the flesh. There is no pain after that, only a numbness, I think." Father Jude gave way to several demented women who, supervised by one of the nuns, proceeded to wipe the floor. The women laughed as they worked. We moved away to the third ward.

Father Jude was correct. I had never confronted such a plague. What if he asked me to treat the illness? For a moment, a great fear froze my intellectual responses to what I was witnessing. I was ignorant of the cause. I had no remedy. I was afraid my medical training was insufficient to deal scientifically with this plague. Nonetheless, I had been sent by his Majesty to deal with precisely these matters of health and I would not let him down. More importantly, I refused to disappoint myself.

The two nuns had guided us to a reception room where another nun waited with food and drink. Father Jude took water and wine. I drank wine, thinking of the possibility of contamination. I was thirsty and had to drink.

Father Jude drank the water. "The plague is concentrated to the South. Thousands of people have perished. It is moving toward the city. The Viceroy wants you to halt its advance."

"Where is the third ward?"

The patients of the third ward were the most atrocious. Upon first seeing them, I prayed to God that they would die almost immediately. *La Mona* had eaten away at their faces transforming them into monstrous mutilations. Those patients with contaminated brains were pitiful, for they smeared their excrement upon themselves and others, they danced with human limbs torn from the corpses in the ward. The violent were kept in a large walled yard next to the third ward. There I observed guards with axes, shovels and clubs, weapons to prevent the insane from escaping. This was not a hospital, it was a death camp where people seemed to be herded to die from an illness I could not cure.

There among the sick walked Papá Damián and Gregorio, who asked the same question that I pronounced.

"What treatment do you provide?" my voice bolted angrily.

"We follow what your institution recommends. We wrap the feet, we administer potions, internally and externally. We induce bleeding and, if these prescriptions fail, we amputate the limbs. But the people still continue to die. Nothing has worked against this monster. People are now refusing to endure an amputation because they know that once they are contaminated with *La Mona*, death is inescapable," Father Jude said softly.

"There must be something more we can do."

"There are the native methods of fighting disease, but they have also failed. If we practice Indian medicine, the Holy Office will accuse us of witchcraft. I certainly would not look any better fried at the stake," Father Jude said. We laughed. The forever smiling nuns waited by the doors to a large dining area where we were to be served. Coming from every wall, the moans and cries still persisted. A scream broke above the constant clamor of suffering.

"An amputation, I suppose," Father Jude said and sat against his chair while a nun placed a bowl of lentil soup before him.

"Just across the garden is the infirmary where the amputations are performed. The surgery is carried out by some of the nuns who have volunteered. The healthier patients help by strapping the patient down and by preparing powerful *aguardiente* to lessen the pain. There are no doctors here."

Father Jude sipped his soup. "Do you see now the state in which we live? Neither the Church nor the Crown has done anything to help," Father Jude said, embittered.

"What about the Viceroy?"

"The Viceroy can only do so much. He has attempted to send doctors here, but they decline to come. They would rather suffer the King's castigation. You cannot blame them. Naturally, they are afraid."

Father Jude pushed his plate away and refused more food. I had not thought about food since the beginning of our journey. He offered a basket of brown bread, but I was still unable to eat anything.

"At least take some bread or you will become ill."

After my refusal, he suggested, "We should leave soon."

"What do you do with the dead?" I had been wanting to inquire.

Father Jude paused, waved me to the window and pointed up to the great chimney stacks towering over the converted church known to all as the Hospital de los Santos Mártires.

Black smoke rose slowly, staining the blue sky with the residue of the lives and perhaps even the souls of these poor people. We followed the blissful nuns to our carriage. As we distanced ourselves from the Hospital de los Santos Mártires, I inhaled the stench from the chimneys which formed an ominous cloud above the earth. The infected cloud sent out appendages which pursued us to the city.

If we could burn in hell, we could surely burn on Earth.

6

If you shared enough time and special events with a person who was a stranger, human nature would break down its defenses to allow you to feel comfortable with that individual. The return to Mexico City with Father Jude proved exactly that point. Tired, we both removed our boots and loosened our belts. Father Jude removed the black veil covering his face and opened a bottle of red wine, which he spilled on his black shirt. His maimed face grew natural to me. It no longer scared nor repulsed me. Father Jude drank long from the bottle and pushed it toward me. After my first drink, I swallowed more and our conversation grew more relaxed and spontaneous.

"I wish to tell you a long story. While I speak, you drink." The priest offered a second bottle.

" ... I do not remember my mother or father. I know we lived in Pátzcuaro. The Jesuits took me in at a very young age. They gave me work, educated and prepared me for the priesthood. But I was never ordained a Jesuit. The expulsion order came only months before my ordination. I could not understand why the Society of Jesus was persecuted and exiled. I had witnessed only good from those men. Soon after the expulsion decree, the people in the country protested the unexpected and cruel decision. Peasants in the provinces and the cities rioted and were accused of plotting to overthrow the government.

"In Pátzcuaro, Pedro de Soria, an Indian chief, led thousands of people in revolt. Most of the villages in his territories were involved, including the city of Uruapan, which was known as a city of resistance to royal and military administration. The rebellion

35

continued for days and several prominent Spaniards were killed, but after it was crushed, peasant blood ran freely through the streets.

"About a week later, José de Gálvez, minister of the Indies, rode into Pátzcuaro determined to make examples of the traitors and those who supported the Jesuits. He immediately sentenced Pedro de Soria and five of his chiefs to death. Gálvez ordered every house in Pátzcuaro to be searched. He found three priests who, whether they were Jesuit or not, he had stripped, flogged and exiled. One priest fought his abusers and was hacked to death by Gálvez's soldiers. I watched this after I had emerged from my hiding place in a stable owned by an Indian *curandero*. He had forced me to prostrate myself in the middle of the stable and he piled dung on top of me until he sculptured what he called in jest a 'living dung heap.' I was saved by excrement." Father Jude wiped his lower lip with his sleeve and handed the bottle back.

"That night when the soldiers were busy abusing the towns-people, the *curandero* took me to a friend, who transported me to Veracruz. In Veracruz, I spent two days when at last I was con-tracted on a Royal galleon packed with the collected taxes of his Majesty's starving subjects. The ship was headed to Cuba, and I to Haiti, where there was great revolutionary activity. I wanted to help the slaves there. We broke anchor at midnight, entered easterly winds and by daybreak no land was in sight. After a few hours, the captain located a speck to the starboard side that traveled parallel with our ship. Noon approached and the speck grew into a ship, now approaching. She was a large battleship with no identifiable markings and, to the crew's great fear, no flag flew from any part of her. The ship was twice as big as ours and sailed fast toward our bow. The captain sounded battle stations. As the men frantically prepared hand weapons and loaded cannons, there came a sense of facing our last battle. The odds were overwhelmingly against us; we had only but our lives to lose. The instant that I could see figures of men moving about on that great pirate battleship, her first cannon volleys crushed our masts; a second volley of cannon fire demolished the captain's quarters. We were crippled almost immediately, floating dead in the water, unable to run, nor steer. French-speaking pirates boarded us on the starboard side. Shooting and slashing, they showed no mercy. We fought, but we were outnumbered. As the massacre raged on, we lowered two lifeboats. Most of our men were killed or wounded and thrown overboard.

"While I helped lower one of the boats, I was hit from the side and turned around. I remember seeing a flash of silver blade cross my sight and feeling a flow of warm blood running from my nose and mouth. I was struck again and pushed head first into a pile of ground corn which had been prepared by the Indian cooks on board. I remember the pirates' laughter as they stood me up with my bleeding face covered with yellow corn meal. They found me comical. They poured more ground corn over my bleeding face and head. The last I remember was being thrown overboard and landing in one of the boats." Father Jude cleared his throat.

Suddenly, not knowing how to respond, I blurted, "Fortune smiled upon you!"

We approached the city, more sick people crowded into the streets, searching for food or a place to die. I gestured to Father Jude to continue his story.

"I opened my eyes somewhere on the gulf coast of Mexico surrounded by Mayan Indians, who nursed me back to health. I lived with a *curandero* and his family for five years. I became his apprentice and he taught me what I know of Indian medicine. During the last year with him, I became the principal practitioner in his village. I realized that if he were to die while I was there, it would be extremely difficult to leave. The village would see me as their *curandero* and I did not want to stay.

"I left and headed for Mexico City where I was taken in by Franciscan monks. No one could refuse me; who could resist not helping this face?" Father Jude sat back and closed his eyes.

He slept amidst the cries of the suffering along the road back to my regal chambers. His head bobbed forward, saliva ran onto

his clothing. I folded a thick linen towel over Father Jude's heart
to absorb his secretions. While Father Jude continued to sleep, I
alighted from the carriage. Before I entered the royal apartments,
I looked to the firmament and witnessed the dark grey cloud from
the crematorium extend its cords of death over the city. Inside, in
the beauty of my rooms, I fathomed deep sorrow and sadness.

7

For five months, Father Jude took me to the clinics and hospitals where I investigated the needs and possible ways of improving the health and medical services in the city. I interviewed doctors, surgeons, pharmacists and a renowned Indian *curandero*. By now I was used to the stench of human waste and death, to the obscene acts on the street and the cruelty and general filthiness of the city and its population. During this time, a serenity of suffering fell upon the people. They seemed to stare out beyond the aqueduct where *La Mona* ravaged the people of the provinces. They were like lost children, fearful, lonely, abandoned by their mothers and fathers. Now only the presence and possibility of death gave them comfort. By the end of the third week of my investigations, *La Mona* had seriously penetrated numerous sections of the city. As I continued to gather statistics, *La Mona* mounted her victory trophies by the hundreds in the streets of the capital. The dead waited for days before the death carts picked them up.

I grew more powerless against her.

My last discussions were with the General Secretary of the Holy Office, Father Juan Antonio Llorente, a doctor, an historian, as well as Father Jude's confessor. In the village of Coyohuacan, he taught surgery to select medical students from the university. Father Antonio, a highly respected doctor and critic of the Holy Office, was one of those unique individuals who could freely comment on the policies of the institution that supported him. Father Jude had warned that Father Antonio initially resisted the interview because he feared that I would prohibit his practice and school. On the contrary, I admired and advocated that activity. We met in a large

parlor decorated with Indian tapestries, rugs, pottery and heavy
furniture; on the tile floor potted flowers lined the whitewashed
adobe walls. The room was cold and a chill grabbed my shoulders
as Father Antonio entered with two young men who then waited at
the door. Father Antonio motioned to us to remain seated.

"Welcome, my son." Father Antonio took Father Jude's hands
and sat directly before me. "You bring a distinguished guest with
you?"

"Yes, Father." Father Jude bowed his head. "Don Gregorio
Revueltas, first doctor of the *Protomedicato*."

"How may I be of service, Don Gregorio?" Father Antonio
rubbed the tips of his fingers.

"Father Jude has explained my mission. I want to know what
you would do to improve medical conditions here in New Spain and
what are the treatments you recommend for *La Mona*." I was ready
with paper and quill.

"Simply stop ravaging the resources of Mexico. Leave monies
here and designate an appropriate amount of funds for medical
services and training. Let the Viceroy know, let the King beware
of the possible decimation of the population. The Indian masses
reproduce at an alarming rate, but even today they are still the
most vulnerable to disease. This plague will kill at least a million
savages. The Holy Office must stop persecuting the *curanderos*,
for they are an asset to us. Many are truly learned *texoxotla ticitl*,
doctors and surgeons. It is not important that they speak Latin.
They save more lives with their vulgar language than we do with our
sanctified words." Father Antonio waited until I stopped writing. I
looked up and he spoke again. "Treatment for *La Mona*? *La Mona*
is not a curable disease. I know of no person who has survived its
painful wrath. We can only wait for it to complete its full course. By
bleeding, medicinal herbs and roots and amputation we can slow it
down, give the patient at most nine months to a year. Here in my
clinic, I train surgeons, specialists in amputations. Please come to
my lyceum. Several of my students are working there now." Father

Antonio smiled and led the way. With trepidation and excitement, I followed.

8

The pungent smell of vinegar made my eyes tear. I counted twenty-five cadavers on tables in a room occupied by nine students. We moved closer to watch two men perform the amputation of the left arm of a female cadaver. Carefully they severed through the *musculus pectoralis major* and sliced down to the humerus bone. The surgeons then cut around the bone and sawed the arm off. The procedure took about an hour. The *arteria* and *vena* were knotted and the wound dressed. Father Antonio congratulated his joyful apprentices for the precise surgery accomplished. The two men were excused. The younger one handed me his scalpel. As they walked off waving the amputated arm to their colleagues, who were working on the left leg of a male cadaver, I recognized who they were. It was Papá Damián and Gregorio, but this vision I kept to myself.

"What my students do is literally map the human anatomy. They are intimately knowledgeable about every organ of the human being. They are taught how to remove and replace every organ," Father Antonio said proudly.

"Has amputation ever been successful against *La Mona?*" I asked as I noticed that on every table there was a body at different levels of dissection. I walked over to a body whose face lacked a nose and lips. I could easily see the *nasalis inferior* and *media*. Father Jude calmly looked down at the dissected face. Why had I approached that cadaver? How insensitive of me. I felt cruel, but no longer saddened. Father Antonio had waited to see Father Jude's reaction. Father Jude turned to him and waited.

"Amputation . . . No, it only slows the progress of the disease. No one survives *La Mona*," Father Antonio said and signaled to his students to stop work. As we left the lyceum, my thoughts were with Father Jude, who walked ahead, and with the cadavers we left behind. I noticed that the smell of vinegar became stronger. My eyes teared more.

That evening we joined Father Antonio for dinner. With hunger satisfied, we rode back to the city after midnight. Father Jude studied the stars. I listened to the constant cries of thousands of mourners. I saw the torches marking the piles of dead. The unbearable smell choked me. Why had I come? I was helpless against all this. My eyes swelled with tears. I sobbed like a child. For an instant I saw Renata's face blurred by a window of tears. I could barely remember her. God, was there no beauty here? No peace, no joy? No love in New Spain? As I walked to my bedchambers I was escorted by a serpent who left me at the door. That night I slept free of visions.

9

One morning I awoke to the realization that I had lived and worked in New Spain for almost three years. I had forgotten the faces of my family and even the face of my sweetheart, Renata. New Spain had engulfed me with a plethora of physical activities, with struggles for survival, both individual and collective. I understood that the saving of these people ensured my physical and mental endurance, and most important the survival of my soul. For me the act of survival in New Spain became an ardent infinite obsession. From the moment I had set foot in this land, I walked with fear. Now I walked with experience and a desire to make the world better. After three years, the city was cleaner, safer. Criminals were punished, the obscenities practiced in public places by the desperate were banned. The clogged drainage systems received attention. More public baths were installed. Fountains were designated for drinking only. Garbage and death carts circulated through the city streets more often. Doctors and surgeons were required to treat all patients; the university medical school opened its doors to treat the indigent. Botanical gardens were laid out in the suburbs of the capital for the entertainment of the people. It seemed that these improvements helped strengthen the population. *La Mona*'s killing had subsided and seemed to be moving away to the North, where I strolled through the gardens of the magnificent Jesuit seminary of Tepotzotlan, not far from the capital.

Since our arrival, Father Jude and I explored the seminary. Its library, classes, dormitories and church were sublime works of art. Here in this baroque complex of carved wood, stone, silver and gold, the viceregal family had lived for almost three years, exiled away from the people and the plague. I enjoyed the rich facade on the single tower, and the great doors carved of stone were impressive. Most astonishing was the interior of the church, with its golden altar and gilt chapels. When the sun shone through the windows and kindled the gold of the *retablos* and altarpieces, a supernatural aura was created. Here in this mystical atmosphere, I waited alone for my friend Don Juan Vicente, the Viceroy, whom I was to see for the first time since I came to Mexico.

Escorted by Father Jude, the Viceroy entered the bright sunlight that flickered and gleamed off his golden coat. Don Juan Vicente's pants, shirt and vest were woven from silk and golden thread. He was a blinding contrast to Father Jude. I laughed to myself at the Viceroy's gaudiness as I stared at his golden slippers. His glittering attire was so bright that I did not go to meet and greet him. The Viceroy responded to my hesitation by sitting next to me. I could not remember him, but finally I saw his face. He appeared old and tired.

"Gregorio, my dear friend. You have done well," Don Juan Vicente said with saddened eyes.

"What are your wishes? I am here to help you," I said. A silence fell while we contemplated the golden light streaming through the windows of the church.

"How is Doña María Alfonsina? Your daughters? Why did you refuse to see me all these years?" My questions made Don Juan Vicente uncomfortable.

"Just a moment, remember who you are. You do not question the Viceroy. However I do recognize your great efforts to improve life in the city and to conquer the plague. For that I will answer your first two questions. My family is well."

Don Juan Vicente took my hand in his. "I have ordered you here because I want you to treat someone who has *La Mona*. Father Jude will take you to her this evening. She is very dear to me. You must save her. My time as Viceroy is coming to an end. The Old World is changing drastically. The New World will follow suit. Now, for you, the most important duty you have is to save the life of this child. I have faith in you. I have faith in your science, Gregorio."

Don Juan Vicente knelt and prayed before the splendid golden altar. Father Jude indicated that I had received my orders and that there was nothing left to discuss. We exited the church and for the first time in months, children frolicked and played under the warm afternoon sun.

10

On the morning of September 15, 1791, the day that Father Jude introduced to me the child I had to save, the sky opened and in less than an hour, tons of water flooded the village of Tepotzotlan. Water was such an inconsistent resource. It was always too much or too little. By noon, the streets were almost dry, no trace of the downpour, the village left clean.

That morning I wrote a short letter to my parents and to Renata, whose letters I seldom correspond. I had dozens of unopened letters. Nonetheless, every week she wrote to me faithfully. It was difficult for me to remember their beautiful faces. In my brief letter I mentioned how much work there needed to be done here. I never told them of *La Mona*, never described the dangers, nor my loneliness. I ended by telling them that I was fine. Often, I thought that Renata should forget me. I wished her parents would release her from her vows to me.

Father Jude came for me at one. We walked to a central garden and through a large field, then through two more large gardens within the seminary compound, surrounded by immense stone walls. Father Jude guided me without hesitation. He knew the location of every pot hole and raised stone, as if he habitually walked these paths. We approached a large residence where two royal guards stood stationed at the entrance. We walked right in and went to a sitting room, next to the kitchen with a small dining table. The smell of pastry and coffee with cinnamon, brown sugar and chocolate floated in from the kitchen. With great informality, Father Jude removed his coat, boots and made himself comfortable at the table.

"Coffee and sweet bread," he ordered.

In a matter of minutes, two Indian women servants brought coffee and cakes. The women freely discussed gossip and the latest news from Spain and other parts of the world, news that they had heard from priest and guests who visited the seminary. I had come to understand that this was Father Jude's home, that these were his servants and friends and that the sick child lived here. I sensed that I needed no introduction. I joined in the discussion whenever I desired. I found the women to be wonderfully funny and perhaps for the first time in years, I laughed aloud. This was not to say that we avoided serious themes. Not in the least. The women's assertions of *La Mona*'s death toll seemed quite complete and accurate. As I listened to one of the women's descriptions of the devastation, I recalled my parents' detailed letters concerning the revolutionary movement and the reign of terror launched by the new political forces of France.

France stood at war with nearly all of Europe and the French were beginning to slaughter one another by the thousands. They, too, stacked their dead in the streets of their capital. They, too, suffered a natural disaster. I thought as I munched my sweet cake and sipped coffee, listening to the political reflections of Father Jude and these two quite intelligent women. After I poured myself a second cup of coffee, the conversation abruptly changed.

"And Laurinda?" Father Jude asked one of the women.

"She is playing in her room. I worry about Marisela. She is so pale and fatigued. I fear that perhaps she too might have *La Mona*," one of the women answered and offered more sweet bread to Father Jude.

The house was comfortable and orderly. It was decorated with common furniture made by Indian and Mestizo craftsmen. Elegance did not describe the atmosphere of Father Jude's home, but rather it was seductively alive with Mexican colors from handwoven blankets, pillows, rugs, tapestries, gabans and more native items. I do not believe that there were any Spanish products in his home. It was Mexican, warm and beautiful. And I felt a strong sense of love.

Father Jude pushed away from the table and in his stocking feet led
me to where Laurinda played.

"Father, your boots! *La Mona* will get you! You are so mulish!"
one of the women yelled from the sitting room.

He waved off her warning and turned into a long corridor with
four doors on each side and at the end, a double door. The doors
opened to a large living room with toys and a magnificent collection
of beautiful dolls. The room had doors with beveled glass that led
to a wonderful garden. Out there, I thought I saw Papá Damián
and Gregorio looking into the center of this delightful place where
Laurinda played, accompanied by a young woman. Throughout
my stay in Mexico, the presence of those two men had constantly
pursued me. My efforts to understand the meaning of the vision were
in vain. Upon seeing Father Jude, Laurinda ran to his embrace. She
was beautiful, her age about seven. The shape of her chin, cheeks
and eyes formed the face of the Viceroy. The young woman was his
mistress, and Laurinda his child. Laurinda's hands and feet where
covered with white silk gloves and slippers.

"Laurinda, this is Doctor Gregorio. He has come to help us,"
Father Jude said and turned to the woman who waited patiently.

"Marisela, Doctor Gregorio Revueltas, director of the *Protomedicato*. He has been sent by the Viceroy."

Marisela came closer, acknowledged the introduction with a
slight curtsy. "Welcome, doctor. We are glad you are here."

Laurinda's beauty was also her mother's. Marisela was tall and
slender, with dark hair and black eyes that I fell into. Was this
the face of Renata? I could not remember. But I was sure that
Renata was as beautiful as Marisela. I contemplated her face as
she apprehensively watched Father Jude remove Laurinda's white
gloves. The child had *La Mona*. Already, her finger tips were
reddish, pulpy and tender. She pulled her hands away when I
squeezed the upper part of her fingers.

"Her feet are the same," Father Jude said softly running his
fingers through Laurinda's silky black hair.

"We must retire, Father," Marisela said. Laurinda grabbed a large cloth doll and dragged it to her bedchambers. I resisted in making the comparison, but the truth was that in months Laurinda would suffer the same fate as the doll.

That night in my room, not far from where Marisela and Laurinda slept, I wrote my treatment plan for the child. I knew that I could prolong the child's life. But saving her was another matter. *La Mona*, I was convinced, would have her way. Nonetheless, I planned phlebotomy, potion and bone treatments. Amputation was my last resort. I closed my notebook and Marisela floated in my mind.

11

Early the next morning, Father Jude and I began treatment. First, we made a light incision completely around each finger and each toe. We allowed the bleeding to continue for an hour. Laurinda did not cry. The scalpels were extremely sharp and the pain caused by *La Mona* was probably greater than the delicate slicing of her fingers and toes. We administered a sulfur ointment to burn away and block the progress of the disease further up the arms and legs. Father Jude dressed the wounds with gauze and placed the white gloves and slippers back on her hands and feet. If this treatment had any affect, we would know within a few days.

That afternoon Father Jude left to minister to the dying in the provinces. I studied in Father Jude's library and constantly monitored Laurinda's condition. Marisela never left her daughter's side and she was ever present in my thoughts. During those two days she helped me with Laurinda's treatment only to reconfirm the relentless nature of the affliction. The disease began to assault the right hand and foot. Tears streamed from Marisela's eyes. She went to the garden. I caught up with her and spontaneously held her while she sobbed.

"I know she is doomed," Marisela said. "I wish it would take her now."

"But we can prolong her life. If we give up, she will surely die in weeks. But if we treat the disease, Laurinda might live a year or more," I said.

"What are you talking about? How can you prolong life?" she asked looking back to where her child played.

51

"Surgery is the only way. If allowed to take its course, the disease will internally eat away Laurinda's arms and legs. If we amputate her hands and feet, it might take months for *La Mona* to take hold of her arms and legs again," I said calmly, hiding my desperation.

"*La Mona* will kill her horribly or she might die from the surgery," Marisela said softly.

"Yes, that too . . . "

"If amputation is to be my daughter's fate, then it must be mine as well, for I must be assured of at least six more months of life," Marisela said and with great modesty revealed her ankles. "I can scarcely walk," she said. Marisela's feet were stained with *La Mona*'s reddish hue.

I continued to apply the treatment to Laurinda and initiated Marisela's. Father Jude returned in two days. I explained to him the urgency of Laurinda's condition and Marisela's state. Although I suggested that we consult Father Antonio Llorente, Father Jude refused. After examining Laurinda and Marisela, he too was convinced that the only way to prolong life was surgery.

The amputations began the following morning. The preparation of Laurinda started after breakfast when Father Jude gave her orange juice combined with *xinaxtli*, a strong fermented maguey syrup. Every half hour thereafter Laurinda was given a dose of the potion.

At one in the afternoon she was primed. Marisela placed Laurinda naked on a high white marble table. With her eyes and mouth open, her respiration ever so slow, Laurinda appeared to be virtually dead. With a pin, I pricked her upper arm. No reaction. Scalpels, saws, thread and tourniquets were made ready. Hot water, lard and linens were brought in by the women servants. To abate the pain, Father Jude applied *iyauthtli*, a grayish-purple cream to Laurinda's arm, shoulder, torso and head. The cream had been extracted from what he called "the lucid mushrooms" given to him by an Indian *curandero*. I noticed that the cream hardened, forming a mask upon

Laurinda's beautiful face.

"You should not stay," Father Jude said to Marisela.

Silence dominated. Marisela did not move. Silently, Father Jude indicated that we should begin. He chose a scalpel. I raised Laurinda's right hand and Father Jude carefully started to cut deep. Although I applied pressure to retard the bleeding, a steady stream persisted. In minutes, Father Jude finished and tied and tucked away two large veins. The bleeding subsided considerably. I stared into his grotesque face and he pushed a saw into my hands. Suddenly I felt that more people were in the room. I searched for Marisela. I needed a sign of assurance that what I was about to do had to be done. I could not swallow, nor speak. Laurinda moved. Father Jude pushed my hands toward the bone. I looked toward Marisela again and found that Papá Damián and Gregorio stood behind her, screaming for me to sever the hand. Marisela nodded slightly. I immediately began to saw through the bone.

"Good work," Father Jude said as he finished applying lard to the linen dressing. He instructed the servant women to administer the *xinaxtli* potion and *iyauthtli* cream every half hour until the next day.

To sleep was impossible. The three of us took turns monitoring Laurinda. At times, the three of us watched as the medicines were given. Although no one else saw them, Papá Damián and Gregorio stood vigil over the sick child.

I went to Marisela who waited in the garden. I did not hesitate to hold her hands, to comfort her. A good feeling overcame my body, soul, life. Oh, God, liberate us! I thought and I embraced her. I realized that I could never understand her courage. With all the scientific knowledge I had, I was unable to relieve her pain. Laurinda cried out and we immediately went to her side. She saw us and her smile shattered the thin mask. She talked about two strange men who spoke to her. She insisted that they were standing next to us wearing strange clothing. Father Jude and Marisela were convinced that she was hallucinating and were not concerned. But to me, Laurinda in her agony had confirmed the existence of my vision of Papá Damián and Gregorio. At that moment she understood that I saw them also.

When we removed the dressings, Father Jude and I were shocked by what we saw. The stump had begun to gather the reddish veil of *La Mona*. We had not cut high enough. The arm was infested with the disease. I screamed from anger and helplessness. I cried for Laurinda and Marisela, and for Laurindas and Mariselas throughout Mexico. We examined her feet and legs and discovered that the disease had progressed even faster and that her left arm also was devastated up to the elbow. She could not tolerate another amputation. Marisela observed everything and understood that her daughter would not survive. Marisela's lips moved in prayer. I prayed that death would come swiftly. We continued to administer the potions and cream. By early morning Laurinda twisted and turned her body. She had to be restrained. The severe pain gave her an abnormal strength that made it difficult to hold her down.

"Let her go until she can go no longer," Father Jude suggested.

Marisela and I released Laurinda, who then writhed about violently. Like a doll, her arms and legs flopped and twisted. She went on to the floor where she squirmed until an hour later the child lay motionless. She called to her mother and finally died.

Father Jude sent word to the Viceroy of Laurinda's death. No response ever came from the Viceroy. The woman servant who delivered the message said that the viceregal household had been in mourning for several days. It was rumored that Doña María Alfonsina had fallen ill with *La Mona* and had taken her own life.

The servant woman reported that in the city and the provinces the death toll of the plague had subsided. People spoke about a possible break in the disease, that perhaps the pestilence was coming to an end. Father Jude, Marisela and I listened and did not respond to the news about the world outside. We prepared to do what we knew had to be done. We celebrated a wake and prayed the rosary for Laurinda, and in the early morning with the sun and birds proclaiming the start of a new day and with Papá Damián and Gregorio present, we buried Laurinda in a small cemetery in one of the gardens of the seminary of Tepotzotlan.

12

It is impossible for me to describe my feelings the night that Father Jude and I examined Marisela. Two women servants were present and rejoiced with Marisela's pregnancy, which advanced in a natural and wonderful way. Several months had passed since we had placed Laurinda into the ground. During Christmas we laughed and played with the promise of new life. I had never before experienced the way our inhibitions abandoned us. Marisela wore a white night-gown. She placed her hands over her belly and laughed at her purple finger tips. She held them up for all of us to see. She wiggled them and reached for Father Jude, who went to her and reassured her that the baby would be born normal. She had advanced well into her pregnancy and the disease seemed to have paused. The baby could come at any moment.

"Do not take my hands from me. I want to hold my baby," Marisela said and sat up on the couch in the living room. "Take my feet. I want to float from earth to paradise. I don't want to walk. I want God to ask me why I am floating on stubs instead of walking on feet. I want to make sure he has not forgotten us."

Marisela raised her feet up for us to examine. The bottoms were purplish grey with streaks of red hue beginning to lace around the ankle and calf muscle. Soon the lower leg would be netted with *La Mona*'s reddish-hued stocking. This could happen at any moment. We were ready to amputate that leg.

In the first week of February, a messenger delivered a bag of mail from Spain. Among the batch of letters were a few from my parents. I opened the most recent and read that rumors in Spain accused the Viceroy of fiscal incompetence and dementia.

In France, Robespierre systematically carried out the execution of thousands of political foes and their allies. In Paris, the knife was not spared and French blood ran through the streets. I placed the letters on my desk, hoping to find time to read and answer them, but I knew that I would not. Earlier that day I had overheard the women in the kitchen mention that *La Mona*'s death rate was diminishing. I prayed for the pestilence to break its grasp on all of us. I had not gone out of the seminary since September of 1791 and now it was early February of 1792. And I would not leave the seminary, I would not leave Marisela alone. My caring for her became an obsession. I realized that I wanted her child and that I would protect the baby.

"Father Jude and you must keep my baby. Raise the child for me. Please do not abandon it. Please do not leave us . . . " Marisela spoke softly.

In the beautiful cold mornings in the Valley of Mexico, I strolled through the gardens of the seminary. Beyond the walls the magnificent volcanos rose to majestic snow white heights. Outside, children played and people walked while discussing the Spring planting. Step by step life gathered strength on the outside. The sound of animals and the laughter of active people slowly overcame the cries of death and the prayers of mourning. *La Mona* was letting go and the populace was living on. Yet inside this imposing seminary, we struggled with death, not to conquer death, but to placate it for time enough to allow a woman to give birth to her child.

On this cool Winter morning, Marisela drank the *xinaxtli* potion without hesitation and applied the *iyauthtli* cream to both her legs which had been overtaken by the disease almost overnight. From a little above the knees to the feet, *La Mona* had crushed the legs and converted them into skinbags of fleshy pulp and pus. Marisela suffered excruciating pain. We had to amputate immediately to prevent *La Mona* from advancing onto Marisela's torso and devouring the child. Perhaps because of her age, Marisela's muscles, tendons and nerves were stronger than her daughter's. Therefore the op-

eration demanded more time and care. Marisela did not seem to
bleed as much, but as we amputated I could see the infant kick and
move. The child protested the agony of the mother. The details
of the amputation are not needed here. I have duly recorded our
procedures in my medical diary. I continued to do this because of
habit, but I often wondered if anyone then or in the future would
care about what happened to us that day. I glanced over to Marisela,
who drank more *xinaxtli* potion.

Several days passed when Father Jude interrupted my afternoon
meal. He sat at the table quietly. I offered, but he said he was not
hungry. In Tepotzotlan, the second week of the month of February
had been beautiful. The village was cool and clean. The crops
flourished deep green. I felt a sense of change steadily permeating
the people. Father Jude did not have to tell me why he came to my
table so saddened. Early that morning I examined Marisela's hands
and discovered that *La Mona* had devoured her arms up to above
the elbow. Here again, we had no choice. I was sure that Marisela
was almost at full term and that she would begin to contract at any
time. But the unpredictability of *La Mona*'s progress forced us to
amputate. She begged us to spare her arms. She wanted most to
hold her child before she died. It was too dangerous now.

"After you finish here, come to the living room and we will
begin," Father Jude said and moved to prepare for the amputations.

Again the cutting through the limbs of Marisela was difficult,
especially the upper left arm which required the use of an ax. We
accomplished what Marisela had dreaded. The floor beneath her
was bloody as well as the table on which she breathed heavily.
Father Jude's eyes swelled with tears. I looked upon what *La Mona*
had created—a distended limbless woman heaving for breath. As
I watched her struggle, a desire to hold her overcame me. She was
cold. I placed my weak arm under her neck and lifted her to my
warm shivering body.

"Take the child now before I die. You must save the child's
soul!" Marisela urged.

Father Jude and I noticed that the stubs of her upper arms had begun to turn reddish grey and that the stubs of her legs were reddish blue.

"We must try to save them both," I said to Father Jude, who shook his head no.

"We cannot. We must wait until she dies. Then we can open her up and baptize the child. That is all we can do," Father Jude said in a tone of defeat. "To save the mother and child? That has never been done before. Our duty is to baptize the fetus' soul." Father Jude went to Marisela and prayed.

Marisela's eyes reached for me. Her eyes implored me to save the child.

"Marisela, you shall see your child. Prepare yourself," I said and called the servant woman who knew that I was about to perform a cesarean. At the time, I did not find it curious that they had been ready, I suppose, for hours. One of the women brought in the instruments. She positioned herself next to me ready to assist. Father Jude prepared to baptize the infant. Nearby, Papá Damián and Gregorio indicated that I had no time to waste.

I reached for my barber's razor, the sharpest scalpel I possessed. With it, I carefully sliced down on the right side and across to the left of Marisela's abdomen. I cut deeper, ever so cautiously, through the uterus, to where I could see a hand, a face, a foot through the membrane of the placenta. I broke the bag of life and the servant women sponged up the water, blood and mucus. With the greatest dexterity that I could bring forth, I reached into Marisela's womb and extracted a live, well-developed girl, whose powerful little lungs bellowed a cry. This initial sound of life was joined by the servant women's rejoicing and Marisela's shriek to see her baby. The servant women assisted me as I cut off the umbilical cord four fingers away from the belly of the infant. I cauterized the cut with a lighted candle. I cleaned the infant's nose of any filth to facilitate breathing.

The servant women introduced sweet water into the infant's

mouth and swaddled her in white cloth. She held the baby for Marisela to see. Marisela opened her mouth wide and moaned calmly.

"Place the child on her chest," I told the servant woman.

She did so, gently. Father Jude, who had completed the sacrament of Extreme Unction during the operation, rejoiced and prepared for the baptismal rite. One of the servant women held the child for Father Jude, who prayed and readied the holy water for the anointing. Marisela seemed to smile as she heard Father Jude's words. I had only looked up to the child for a short while, but in that instant Marisela left us.

"In the name of the Father, the Son and the Holy Ghost, I baptize you Mónica Marisela."

A transcendent emotion of pride from the woman who had just given birth to her daughter converted my tears into joy and resolution.

13

Have you ever felt terribly alone and yet strangely warm and happy? That was the emotion that I experienced the day Father Jude, Mónica Marisela and I, along with three servant women, interred Marisela next to Laurinda in the beautiful garden cemetery in Tepotzotlan. Even now that loneliness rushes through my physical and mental being.

I remained in Tepotzotlan caring for Mónica Marisela, watching her grow healthy and strong. It seemed as if with her birth, *La Mona*'s attacks on the populace had dwindled to nothing. By April of 1792, no new cases of *La Mona* had been reported. For two months I commuted once a week to Mexico City, continuing to work with the medical faculty at the university. Father Jude carried on his work with the poor and sick. But more and more, his trips were further away and longer. His most recent trip was to a jungle area south of the city. He returned badly congested, feverish and weak. The village where he had worked had been engulfed by a plague of mosquitoes. After that trip, Father Jude changed. He spoke very little. He hardly ate. He wandered about the seminary alone and I often found him standing or sitting next to Laurinda's and Marisela's graves. I suppose he had been like a father to them. I, too, felt their absence, but I worked through my loneliness and often rejoiced with Mónica Marisela in my arms. I labored for a better world, a better Mexico for Mónica Marisela. I sensed a new attitude toward life grow within the people. University professors and students conversed about freedom and equality, about rationalism and liberalism. Intellectuals declared that human beings should no longer be oppressed by the trinity of the king, the priest and the landed aristocrat. They proclaimed that governments should be based on the consent of the people, that religion should be a private matter, that society should no longer be divided into hereditary classes, that a person should rise as high as talent would carry him. These ideas soon circulated amongst the folk. In the streets, in churches and in taverns, I heard the people discuss the future of their country.

In June of 1792, as I witnessed Father Jude grow stubbornly older and weaker, a captain and an eight-man escort of his Majesty's Royal Guard invaded the peaceful afternoon at Tepotzotlan with a request that I accompany the Viceroy, Don Juan Vicente de Guemes Pacheco de Padilla, Count of Revilla Gigedo, to Veracruz, where one of his Majesty's galleons awaited for his return to Spain. My initial thought was not to go, but the captain's demeanor forewarned dire consequences if I refused.

The royal petition was accompanied by a letter which did not bear his Majesty's Royal Seal. The letter came from Havana. I immediately recognized Renata's hand. She was to arrive in Veracruz on the 15th of June, on the ship that brought the new Viceroy. It was the same ship on which my friend Viceroy Don Juan Vicente, disgraced and demented, was to return to the mother country.

The third time I saw Don Juan Vicente was on the day of our departure. Wearing the glittering gold suit which he had worn the last time I saw him, he appeared tired and bizarre. He and his oldest daughter spoke incoherently. Father Jude explained that Doña María Alfonsina had fallen ill with *La Mona* and had chosen to take her own life rather than suffer a prolonged death. The Viceroy's youngest daughter, after discerning that *La Mona* had seized her body, had ventured into the jungle and disappeared.

The rainy season came on fast, making the trip to Veracruz slow. I worried about Renata, but could not remember her face. Throughout the journey I concentrated on the hardened mask of unbelievable terror and sadness lacerated on the Viceroy's and on his daughter's faces. Their cruel lot grotesquely grew on their faces and bodies. We were lucky to have made Veracruz a few days before the ship was scheduled to leave. Supplies for the return trip had arrived late and the crew continued to load the precious cargo destined for Spain. As he walked up the gangplank of His Majesty's Ship Godoy, a heavily armed galleon, I finally said goodbye and released Don Vicente's hand. Perhaps at that instant he recognized me and understood what had occurred.

He smiled slightly, looked at his wet golden coat and boarded. While I listened to his official "thank you," the escort captain handed me an envelope which contained a voucher for a coach to Mexico City and a note indicating that Renata waited at the Hotel Colón there in Veracruz.

14

To see Renata was not an easy decision. I at least owed her the courtesy of acknowledging her visit to New Spain. I dared not think that she had come in search of me, but there was no other reason for her presence.

For the past four years, I had been guilty of neglecting the woman to whom I had been promised. And guilty as well of neglecting my dear mother and father. I had been guilty of neglecting my life in Spain. But it was amusing to think that my concerns were no longer of life in the Old World, but of life here in Mexico. Four years ago on my arrival, it would have been absurd to think that I would consider remaining and working in Mexico. At that time, I did not have the wonderful gift of Mónica Marisela. I rehearsed reasons to explain my refusal to return to Spain. Renata had endured the trip to Mexico to convince me to go back with her. Still, it was not my fault. She should have written that she was coming. I laughed out loud at the absurdity of me reading letters. How cruel of me, I thought, as I waited in the garden of the Hotel Colón. I was afraid that I would not be able to recognize her. Suddenly, to my eyes, my throat, my mouth there rushed tears and a cry which I stifled into a feigned cough into my handkerchief. The waiter noticed my discomfiting state and poured more tea. The sweet smell of cinnamon reminded me of my house in Tepotzotlan, the three women servants, Father Jude and my beautiful child Mónica Marisela, people I loved and would never leave. And this time I cried out loud and drank the hot tea in a futile attempt to regain my composure, for there before me appeared out of the white walls of the Hotel Colón, Renata, the woman to whom I was betrothed.

To Renata's right, a young Indian woman played exquisitely on a harpsichord a delightful melody which described every movement which Renata made as she came ever closer to me—so near that I could reach out and touch her. I held back in fear that I might obliterate her image, her presence, her body. The Indian woman knew that love had still survived and persisted between Renata and me. The music intensified in beauty as Renata waited for my disbelief to subside.

"I do have your letters," I exclaimed stupidly, not knowing what to say.

Nearby sat a blind man with two dogs and several kittens at his feet. Listening, never blinking, the man appeared to write every word pronounced by Renata and me. He staunchly held a tireless unsatiable quill. The musician played, the writer wrote, and Renata waited against the cool clean white walls of the rain soaked Hotel Colón in Veracruz, Mexico. I reminded myself of where I was, but still could not gain control of the emotions that bewildered my mind, heart and soul upon seeing her sitting so near to me now. I placed my hand over my mouth, for I was afraid she would disappear if I blurted out any more inane confessions.

"Renata are you really here?"

Renata pulled my hands away from my face and forced me to look into her eyes. That night the musician played, the writer wrote and Renata and I talked until the cockcrow hours of the morning.

15

The sweet taste of cinnamon lingered on the tip of my tongue as I walked to Father Jude's grave and remembered my beloved Renata. She had left, weeks ago, on His Majesty's Ship Godoy. I remember Renata's perfectly manicured hand waving from the deck. Next to her stood Don Juan Vicente wearing his golden suit. I did not wait long on the dock. I waved once and walked away from Renata's and Don Juan Vicente's Spain. I returned to my home in Tepotzotlan to be told that Father Jude had died peacefully in his sleep. I held Mónica Marisela and strolled in the Gardens of the seminary and at every step I found Father Jude. My stomach felt empty and sick.

I returned to the house where the servant women with sorrowful eyes went about doing their work. I needed them, I cared for them and I wanted those Indian women to stay. I went to the back portal which lead to the street. I removed the beam from across the doors and swung them wide open.

The servant women came with Mónica Marisela to see the street covered with flowers in honor of Father Jude. Across the street Papá Damián and Gregorio placed a bouquet of roses on the pile of offerings. People smiled and said hello. I kissed Mónica Marisela and I heard liberation in her innocent giggle, which offered a new century in my new country. The afternoon sun passed over my face; perhaps that was the cause of the tear running down my cheek; perhaps it was an older, more ancient tear, traveling through those who had come before me.

Book Two

DELHI

1

The heroic green-blue cypress has stood there ever since I can remember. The behemoth tree was like pure delicate crystal: forever in danger of being broken, cut down by men and women concerned more with industrial profit than the preservation of natural life. The autumn Santana winds arched the sun above and crowned the great cypress with rays of light. I looked up to the top lost in the sun. Here, next to this well-planted tree, I felt rooted in this earth. I danced by the little rivulet that meandered down to what once was my family's home, my *barrio*, Simons. I returned often to stand under the cypress that had known generations of my kinfolk, the people I loved. I came back to fuel my memory.

At night, in spring, summer, autumn and winter I walked round the dancing cypress, found tranquility, closed my eyes and dreamed. Habitually, a multitude of wings or the pandemonium of the city shattered my reverie with nature, but always the cypress endured, peacefully guarding and supporting the sky. Today beneath the cypress' constant gaze and embrace of the world, I found myself in a social position radically different from my parents, Octavio and Nana! They taught me to walk through the past to live in the present and to work for a better future.

Suddenly, as if in a dream, I had become a doctor. And just as suddenly, in a modern Orange County theater, in a crowded hall, my eyes met hers.

In her presence, the cypress spoke to me. "There is magic in her."

I saw the world, the sea, the mountains in her legs, her arms, her face. The cosmos became her body. She smiled. I had seen her somewhere before. Transparent, I panicked and asked her name.

"Sandra," she said.

Sandra and I walked together through a crowded gallery of sounds: wine pouring, glasses clinking, chatter. Laughter and words addressed to her. I sensed her confidence, her powerful identity, and I felt relaxed. She took a cup of coffee without paying. I placed three dollars on the counter. The host pushed it back.

"Have a great performance," he said to her.

Comfortably we stood together. Afraid to respond, I watched her stir cream into the coffee. Her green-blue eyes saw mine.

"And your name?" she asked in a warm open tone.

I reached for my name and found it at the brink of my lips.

"I'll see you after the performance, Gregory," she said and disappeared into the enchanted forest of people. The lights dimmed and the corridor emptied slowly.

At my seat, I fumbled through the program to find the cast, and from a photograph she smiled at me again, Sandra Spear. She was an actress. Beneath the stage lights I listened and watched, hoping to recognize a sign in her voice, in her gestures. But only once did I feel that she actually saw me.

After the performance I waited in the gallery where I had first seen her. In minutes I was by myself. Sandra probably said that to everyone, I thought. I felt foolish, stupid, still believing in fairy tales. Life isn't like the movies, I thought. I headed for the door.

"Gregory!"

In an instant Sandra Spear had changed my life.

2

The Santa Ana medical clinic was located on Staton Street, next to the Catholic church in an old Santa Ana *barrio* called Delhi. This *barrio*, like many scattered throughout Southern California, was built a long time ago to house company workers. This *barrio* had been founded by agricultural laborers who had toiled in the fields and in the Delhi Sugar factory.

The *barrios* of Southern California, the real Aztlán, the origins of my Indian past, shared in common the kind of housing built. The well-tended flower gardens, the beautiful faces marked by the history of young and old Chicanos who worked, studied, loved, hated and helped each other in times of need, and just as easily shot each other to watch a brother or sister bleed to death on the pavement. For revenge, for the reputation of my sister, for a bad drug deal, for pride, for the honor of family, for their *barrio*, the homeboys and homegirls would explain as they lay dying from a huge hole made by a 357 magnum bullet fired from a cruising car at eleven-thirty at night, just when the party was underway.

The results of drive-by shootings, usually gang related, unfortunately had become too common since I had started here three years ago. I could patch the physical wounds. But if the person died, I couldn't deal with what he or she left behind. The toughest part was when I had to face the family. In their faces I saw my mother, father, brothers and sisters. Each time I left a cadaver on the slab, I felt that I had forsaken myself. I could not understand why I ached with guilt!

All night I had danced with death. But I enjoyed my job. Now at seven in the morning I waited for Sandra. She drove from her apartment, two miles away, near the Orange County Theater where a year ago we had met.

Sandra usually sensed when the night had brought bloody business. This morning she knew for sure. We had planned a late evening supper: a light, health-above-taste meal popular in narcissistic health-conscious Orange County. I was to have gotten off at ten last night, but our plans were altered when the bleeding *barrio* warriors began to arrive.

In a new green, twelve-cylinder Jaguar, Father's gift to *his* daughter, we drove to Sandra's apartment.

From the balcony, the San Bernardino mountains rose covered with snow. The morning was brisk, clear. As a child those mountains were so far away, unattainable. But now in a matter of two hours I could walk through forest, ski slopes and drive through their winding roads.

Sandra studied her script.

The apartment was decorated with both modern and ancient objects from North and South America. Sandra had studied in Costa Rica her junior year and traveled from Central America to Tierra del Fuego. In spite of the mortification of her parents, she visited Cuba to attend the Latin American Film Festival. Mexico was her favorite country.

"How do you feel this morning?" I asked.

She put the play down.

"Never better," she said and flung open her arms. We kissed and nothing mattered.

3

I moved through the world like my vision moved over Sandra's body, amazed that she had spoken to me after the performance, forever bewildered that she had chosen me! With Sandra next to my heart, I held the cosmos.

"With all its beautiful smiling stars wearing sombreros and cheering for Sandra Spear!"

Sandra laughed at the silly joke and stretched out relaxed before me, a feast. I wondered how she really felt. The curly pubic locks of her womb clustered upward like our favorite sunny postmodern plaza of massive glass buildings and white-walled parking structures. They formed a canvas on which the sun's light casted forth shadows from a stone pyramid, an immense steel sun dial, a twisted iron sculpture, that demanded at least a passing thought. I loved that stone plaza of artistic monoliths and our favorite continental Mexican restaurant the way I loved her body.

For hours, Sandra and I played in the sun and at night we strolled mystified by the power the flood lights had over us. We danced, and at first made shadow sculptures with our hands, then with our bodies, and bolder yet, together, ever so close together.

Sandra pushed me away, "You're insane."

"And so are you for hanging around with me," I answered and she turned toward me.

I looked down from her eyes and found her breasts like sacred shrines of memories from which I suckled the past. There were two churches that seemed to be important in my life. One was Our Lady of Mount Carmel, the Simons Church, where Father Charles attended to his "wild savages." In that church I was baptized, made

73

my First Communion and my Confirmation. I spent practically a fourth of my youth participating in activities organized by the Catholic Church. I think the Mother Church expected to extract from us at least one priest. To our mother's chagrin, not one guy from Simons ever expressed interest in the priesthood. We were "hoods" and we wanted to screw girls.

Sandra kissed me. "I think you imagine all these things."

"I'll take you to the exact place where the church stood."

The second important church was the United Anglican Church of Whittier. We arrived late for her uncle's wedding. That was the first time I met her parents. They immediately made me uncomfortable. They were both blond. But Sandra's brown naturally curly hair, where did it come from?

In our rush I sat next to her father and she took the aisle. The music began. It was not the traditional American wedding march. It sounded almost Asian. Her uncle came in from the side entrance and on his head was her brown very curly hair. Down the aisle marched a stunning Asian woman.

Sandra's father cleared his throat. "I just don't know about these mixed race marriages. He's the first one on your side of the family to . . . "

"Shut up and stand, Bill!" Sandra's mother firmly ordered.

A bigot and a superwoman, I thought, and I placed my hands on Sandra's shoulders. Without delay, Bill started to clear his throat again.

"Yes, I remember. My uncle and Sashi still live in Japan," Sandra said.

She pushed her curly hair back and her breasts became temples where the mysteries of blood and desire resided. My gaze covered her with red flowers like a spreading bougainvillea covering the walls of a city lapped by the ocean, her body and mine: the two halves of a love. We heard the crystalline song of the fountain in the plaza, the chirping of birds just outside the window, and we embraced with the warmth of the morning sun shining through the slightly opened blinds.

I, ugly and imperfect. Sandra, perfect and beautiful. I loved her for that and for choosing me.

4

Sandra dressed in the color of my most decadent passion and desires. She lived in my common and guilt-ridden male thoughts. She resided naked there in my mind. I tried desperately to shake her off, but she came back and smiled before my eyes. I understood that I had succumbed to her beauty and intelligence. I washed my hands with her, I bathed my body with her, I drank her in the coolness of the cypress tree where I knew that I could not escape her. I thought this when we walked by the warm houses in Delhi.

Clemente, an ancient man that we went to see, lived in an old dilapidated house. Sandra had always wanted to meet him. He had a two hundred-pound jaguar as a pet. The portliness of the sacred cat gave it a cheshire look. Strange as it might seem, the City of Santa Ana did not disturb this kind and gentle beast. Sandra and I watched the jaguar drink water.

"He drinks dreams," Sandra said.

Clemente, happy that we had come to visit him, said, "Only in your eyes."

In Clemente's garden, as in my Mother's, there flew hundreds of butterflies and hummingbirds. The butterflies came and landed on our clothes and the hummingbirds orbited around us like spheres of color.

As evening approached, my eyes passed over Sandra's forehead and traced the path of the moon that rose full above the balcony of her apartment. Sandra slept on a cloud hovering over Orange County, California. I traveled easily through Sandra's womb, as I did through her dreams, and I found that her face had been transfigured into the face of a serpent made up of two great serpents. She dressed in odd clothes that I had never seen before. She wore a singing skirt of undulating fields of corn. Her skirt became crystal and water. Although I tried, I failed to drink. Her lips, hair and desperate eyes rained all night as I lay next to Sandra Spear. That was the first night that she opened my chest and exposed my heart to her pain. But Sandra lovingly closed my eyes with her mouth and covered my opened chest with her bosom of roots, water and love. That night as I fell asleep, I saw above Sandra the green-blue cypress with its dripping roots exposed.

I passed my hand over Sandra's figure and moved on a swift river racing by windows of memory. The victims of the holocaust saw through her bones as her body turned into a forest where we both ran on a path in the mountains. There were two other Jews in my life. Andrea, who while we had made love recalled the horrors suffered by her grandparents. Dr. Milton Flink, who had suffered the abuses against children in the Nazi concentration camps while he watched his parents wither away and die. Flink was the founder of the physician's group to which I belonged. He had treated Sandra the first time I had to rush her to the clinic. She had cut her finger while opening a cardboard box filled with scripts to read. She was so excited at the possibility of reading several roles highly recommended by the director at the Orange County Theater that she ripped the cardboard apart and deeply slashed the palm of her left hand. Only after she had tried every possible way to stop the bleeding did she concede to go. I suspected something when she violently refused my treatment. As we drove to the clinic, I knew then what Sandra admitted to Flink later.

On that short drive, her white shorts and her "Viva La Revolución Cabrones" t-shirt were stained with blood. Sandra bled like a faucet I could not shut off. Flink carried her into the clinic as dark eyes watched in awe. She collapsed as her roots rushed blood to the gash in the dam.

Flink and I saved Sandra for her father and mother. Bill and Phyllis traded her car, with the front seat still soaked in blood, for a new Jaguar and came to cheer her up. Sandra's parents were not surprised to find me at her apartment. First chance Bill had, he spoke his peace. He held nothing back.

"Can't you take better care of her! What kind of a doctor are you, anyway?" He threw the fifty-five thousand dollar keys on the dining table.

Bill and I fell into an unending abyss. We both traveled through her thoughts, somehow sharpened by her physical condition. When they left, the four of us knew we loved each other like a family. Forever I hold that moment dear to my heart. For on that day Bill and Phyllis realized that Sandra and I were lovers. From that day on we were more honest with each other.

5

On a silent afternoon I pushed away from her white forehead as Sandra slept soundly, peacefully in her pale countenance. Finally, my breath came back and I stood against the setting sun and saw my shadow shattered on her Peruvian rug. I struggled to recapture my fragmented being, piece by piece. I proceeded without an essence. I clothed my invisible body. I kissed her and searched through dark corridors, through the infinite paths of memory, and opened the doors to one of the examining rooms in Flink's clinic.

Upon a surgical table there rotted away a mangled female body of summer. Within her fifteen years of angelical pubis grew the jewel of her love for her homeboy who stood nearby, eager to know if she was going to make it.

A tattoo ran along her rib, "My Sacred Heart for Jimmy of Delhi," punctuated with a red arrow pointing to her heart and an unexpected bullet puncture. Jimmy took her hand while I examined the child's uterus and the fetus.

"About six months?"

"You better save her and the baby!" challenged Jimmy. The police guard restrained him.

Her face was pale like Sandra's in the afternoon. Sandra's face disappeared as I labored to save her. Blood trickled down her fingers to the floor. First a drop, then two, and suddenly Flink stepped in the puddle.

"I'm sorry, Jimmy, but her parents refuse permission," Flink said.

"I'm the father!" Jimmy screamed.

"But you're only sixteen." The policeman pushed Jimmy toward the door.

"But I'm the father!" Jimmy's screams were finally silenced by the rush of a police car engine which rapidly faded away.

"She's gone."

"And the baby?"

"A few hours and the fetus will die."

Flink unfolded a sheet.

"We can save the child," I countered.

"The parents don't want it. Their daughter is a hopeless addict. The child is probably as damaged as she."

Flink pulled the white sheet over the mother and placed his hand on her uterus. The similarities of the dead woman's tattoo and the serial number branded on Flink's forearm were unavoidable.

"Maybe less," Flink said and walked out of the room.

A moment later, I heard the wail of a woman and before me, under a white sheet an unborn fetus wrenched in the diminishing oxygen of its dead mother's expiring womb. For an instant the girl's tumultuous hair caressed my hand and became a shiver of scurrying spiders over my sudden deep-felt smile. I fought off tears that night and returned to Sandra to cry with my lips upon her white forehead. She understood and her smile, like lightning, broke the perilous tempest. Her face, like glowing rain, guided me in the dark garden of modern delights. Sandra was like warm rushing water full of life at my side.

6

During this time in our relationship I started to write. Alone I wrote about the falling days, months. A year passed. It seemed as if Sandra had stabilized. But I lived constantly on guard, knowing that at any moment she could fall into the abyss of illness.

Our life, like a road of mirrors, reflected our broken image. We refused to look down. Our vision was forever forward. I walked with Sandra, proudly overcoming the lurking doubts, insecurities of our shadow. She and I lived in search for an instant of security.

Perhaps we found it in the birds singing in the afternoon sun, at about five in the afternoon, that time of which poets sing. Our love was tempered by the glass walls of majestic postmodern buildings among which we strolled, our love tempered by our parents, who reminded us to be careful with each other's hearts. We did not pay attention. We grew in our passion and we conceived.

"Sandra, marry me," I proposed.

"Yes," Sandra whispered, "but wait till after the baby is born."

Happiness was transformed into the precarious task of protecting Sandra's life and the child she carried. Everything came to a halt. She stayed in bed guarding the maturing branch of our love. Four months she lay still, feeling her uterus expand with life.

Sandra wanted to sit in the balcony, look out toward the hills, the mountains, and so I helped her get out of bed. After almost five months we decided she could at least walk a few yards from our bed. It was scarcely ten minutes that Sandra had sat down to enjoy the afternoon breeze.

"I feel wet," she said.

I looked down. The red rose within her had burst like a river. We saw our blood spread over the white tile on the balcony. Somewhere down below us the laughter of young girls embraced us at five on that autumn afternoon.

In the white space of the hospital we lost the child and the bleeding ceased. Surrounded by the beauty of Sandra's curly hair, her transparent face greeted me. When she was out of danger I accompanied Bill and Phyllis to their car. We hugged and standing very close to one another, Bill spoke softly to me.

"Why do you insist on making her suffer?"

As they drove away, a red hue began to slide across the sky. The sun returned with the start of another day.

7

After the movie we went to a Mexican restaurant in Santa Ana, near the Orange County Jail. Radiant paintings of Mexican Indian motifs hung on the restaurant walls. Images of pyramids, volcanoes, sun calendars, warriors and animals. Sandra had physically recovered, and I thought I had found in her face the reflection of a Jaguar roaming the spaces of night. Her green-blue eyes fixed perfectly into my own almond-shaped brown ones. In an instant she possessed all faces, time and places, none of which were familiar to me, yet I knew them all. I remembered the cypress filled with birds, the great star dancing above, chasing away the clouds of winter. She was a priestess and she drank a cup of blood and raised a sword to the sky and violently thrust it through my soul. Her fingers had grown like roots, penetrated and entwined through my body and soul. She asked about my family. Sandra hardly knew them.

My Mother, after my father had passed away, learned to live alone. My older sister Micaela lost her husband about four years ago. My sister Flor's husband died about six months before we met. The women in my family lived without men. Yes, my sisters had children but they lived independent lives. My brother Javier, a relatively happy man, lived with his wife. His sons and daughters kept the family growing. Sandra knew I loved my family. She also knew that I had ambiguous feelings about my oldest brother, Arturo.

"Why don't you go see him?" Sandra asked.

"The only time he shows up is when someone dies," I said.

"You're being as stubborn as he."

Arturo had dropped out of school at a very young age and had never learned to read and write nor do basic mathematics. I was

convinced that he was dyslexic, but never diagnosed. He was a
ladies man. He had many girlfriends: Laura, La Mimy, Tonia,
etcetera. It didn't make much difference to him what their names
were.

Upon his return from Korea, he had an affair with a girl named
Eloisa, whom he dated for several weeks and promised to marry.
Eloisa became pregnant and Arturo abandoned her. Eloisa gave
birth to a boy and named him Michael. Soon after the birth of his
son, Arturo met Casilda, the girl of his dreams, and he married her.
Eloisa sued Arturo. The court ordered Arturo to pay child support
until Michael was eighteen years old.

Eloisa had always told her son that his father had died in Korea.
Michael began to ask for photographs of his father, for evidence of
his death. Finally, he understood that his father was alive and he
insisted on knowing his identity. Eloisa had no choice and told her
son the truth. Through a mutual friend of Arturo's and Eloisa's who
had maintained contact with both, Michael found out the names of
his grandparents and where they lived.

On a spring day, approximately twenty years later, while I was at
the medical school in Guadalajara, my mother Nana and my father
Octavio worked in the rose garden in front of our house, on Español
Street. The Revueltas home was built on the hill that overlooked
the 245 acres where Simons *barrio* used to be located. A young
man approached my parents. Michael in search of his lost roots,
his father. My father and mother did not refuse him his identity, nor
their welcome. The boy returned several times until one day it so
happened that Arturo arrived during one of Michael's visits. Arturo
immediately recognized Michael, but he backed away and refused
to talk to his son.

Casilda accused my parents of undermining her marriage. She
charged them with arranging meetings of Eloisa and Arturo. From
that day, Arturo abandoned the house. He did not speak to my
parents for about two years. He and Casilda gradually severed
relations with everyone on the Revueltas side.

Casilda and he treated Javier, Micaela and Flor terribly. If they would call, Casilda informed them that Arturo did not want to speak to them. If they went to visit, Casilda made them feel unwanted and insulted them by never acknowledging their presence. Arturo never attempted to put a stop to her bizarre behavior. He never tried to defend himself before his family. His children were helpless. They witnessed the loss of their uncles and aunts, but worst of all, the loss of Octavio and Nana Revueltas. Casilda and Arturo had banished their children from their grandparents.

When I returned from Mexico I went to visit my brother Arturo. He was my childhood hero. I looked up to him. He bought me my first bicycle. I loved him and did not want to lose him, nor beautiful Casilda and my nephews and nieces. I arrived at their house while Arturo was washing his car. Casilda came out, recognized me and immediately went back inside. I could hear the children in the back yard; after a short while I heard one of my nephews ask, "But why, Mom?"

Silence and then I heard a door slam. Arturo spoke hurriedly. I remember he did not embrace me. I wanted to hold my brother close to my heart, for only a few seconds, the way we always had expressed our love for one another. But instead we exchanged banal words. Arturo was gone and I remained standing in the center of a black asphalt driveway.

At that moment, like now, recalling that part of our lives, I hoped for revenge, but I never could hurt Arturo. I wondered if he understood how much he had hurt our mother and father.

"Don't be bitter," Sandra said.

8

While Sandra slept, I read her face, her skin, each line, minute pore, fine hair. She had become the text I loved. I wrote about her, Arturo and my family. My writing became fire running over the crevasses of my memory, running over those I loved and those I hated. In sleep and in orgasm with her eyes closed and me desperate over and in her, wanting in some mad way to be swallowed by her. I could not help myself. I could never say no to Sandra.

There were instances when my sight caught a pursued adolescent aspect on her face. I was afraid of the beast that roamed near her, of the days that fell around us, of the walls that surrounded us, of the balcony she loved, of her name, Sandra. I was afraid of losing her.

My fear became desperate when Sandra cried alone. I never went to her. I listened and I cried. I felt a force heavy on my heart push up to my eyes. There was nothing before me, only the instant that I rescued this night, like many others that fell in our bed, sculptured with dreams and the memories that I typed onto the pages of our story. Outside, an Aztec god ascended and pierced my eyes with the gift of a pristine day.

In Orange County, late one morning, Flink sent me to the hospital to see several patients. As I signed off on the charts I was approached by Termolino N. Trompito, TNT, Director of the Hospital Administration and arch enemy to the Flink concept of indigent care in the County. He was nice enough, although through the years I learned that he was unpredictable. He practiced a convenient, power-hungry politics which in the long-run always supported his fellow cronies and above all made him look good. He was about five feet tall with a lofty superiority complex. TNT watched as I put down my last chart.

"How is the clinic progressing?"

I chuckled as I looked down at the little Hitler, who from under his precisely trimmed moustache waited impatiently for an answer.

"You should come and see for yourself, Mr. Trompito."

As I walked out into the city of Santa Ana, the Spanish, the English, names, smells and tastes reminded me that I had promised to visit Doña Rosina. Although she lived only several houses from the Flink clinic, she was unable to walk there. Diabetes had crushed her legs. Suffering great pain, she continued her amazing patch-work art.

Doña Rosina's house was painted to reflect her art. It probably had twenty-five different colors. The garden was manicured and the potted flowers swayed in the slight wind. I knocked. The door opened and before me there appeared the quintessence of female *cholismo*. Her hands were decorated with black rubber-bands woven like spider-web gloves from her fingers up to her wrists. The rubber-bands were as black as her blond-rooted, long full hair which fell freely down her back. She was an oblique specter of colors; her sharp obsidian eyes highlighted with soft shades of grey, white, brown, contrasted with the rectangular blush spot on her cheeks. She wore white baggy pants and a large, striped white and black jersey. She stood her ground until Doña Rosina called.

"Let the doctor come in, *m'hija*."

Doña Rosina worked in the kitchen. She already had a cup of coffee poured and Mexican sweet bread on the table for me. She worked on a large quilt which had the image of the *Virgen de Guadalupe*.

"Come here, *m'hija*," Doña Rosina said.

The young woman came to her side. Doña Rosina reached to her shoulder.

"Doctor Gregorio, this is my niece, Keli, from Ciudad Juárez. She is going to take care of me."

I nodded in agreement and took out my stethoscope to examine Doña Rosina. Through the examination she kept on working. She was approximately eighty-five years and slowly dying of the complications of diabetes. Her legs were swollen and she had an infected ingrown toenail.

"No, don't touch my toes. I won't let you cut them off," Doña Rosina said sternly and reached for Keli, who looked at her aunt's feet with a grimace.

"But, *tía*, it's terrible!" Keli knelt and helped put on Doña Rosina's socks and slippers.

Doña Rosina was determined. "No. I want to die whole." She kept working.

As I prepared to leave, Keli dropped her guard and talked to me confidentially, indicating that she would try to convince her aunt to cure that toe. She understood what the consequences might be. Nonetheless, we understood what Doña Rosina wanted.

Outside, three homeboys arrived. They came to clean and tend the yard. The three youths wore light, quilted jackets with the image of the *Virgen de Guadalupe* on the back. Doña Rosina not only had made the jackets for the Delhi homeboys, but for many years had taken care of them when they were in trouble. She had bailed them out of jail and tried to steer them away from drugs and violence. She had adopted and loved them as if they were her own. By her actions Doña Rosina had become the mother of *Barrio* Delhi.

"Here, take this to Sandra." She handed me a jacket which was like a kaleidoscope of the *Virgen* on cloth. As I looked at the jacket, the multidimensional image of the *Virgen* emanated by the thousands from the weave.

The three young men worked in the front yard. Keli walked me to the door.

From the kitchen table, where she continued to create her magic jackets, Doña Rosina said, "Doctor, you like my colors? They are my children's. Don't ever forget, you are the color of the future. We are the color of tomorrow."

9

The helicopter hovered over the US Embassy in Saigon. People scurried up ladders. Suddenly, the chopper pushed away, several men fell; others clung to life and freedom. This was the scene on television when the Communist forces overran South Vietnam and forced the United States to engage in an immediate evacuation of troops, civilians and Vietnamese refugees loyal to the United States and fearing for their lives. This day marked the end of two decades of military involvement in Vietnam. We had lost the war to skinny, half-naked, rat-eating Vietnamese, who had enormous hearts and guts to match. It was their country now, no question about it.

It was right about this time that Sandra's career began to move upward. She got four important roles, one after another, that kept her working right up to about the middle of November.

The Orange County Theater debated on performing a Spanish play. The administrators were not convinced that their public would enjoy something from Spain, so they dropped the idea. On November 20, Generalissimo Francisco Franco died and the next day Sandra suggested three plays by Federico García Lorca. They selected "Blood Wedding" and Sandra was selected to perform the role of the "bride." She brought the play home for me to read.

"Blood Wedding" was a play about people driven uncontrollably to their death by passion and love. When I finished reading the play, I did not want Sandra to play the role, but she started to rehearse and I soon felt, strangely, that she was born for the role. Long ago she had memorized the play completely and had dreamed that someday she would play the bride. She pronounced every word as naturally as if Lorca heard them. Her face expressed both peace

89

and a deep hurt. Her body moved gracefully through the bride's world.

"I know Lorca," she said. "I know how he felt."

"But will the audience?" I asked.

"Anyone can feel Lorca," Sandra said.

In early January of 1976, two weeks before the opening night of the play, Sandra set out to demonstrate the power of Lorca's poetry. She performed parts of the play to Don Clemente, his jaguar, Doña Rosina, Keli, Flink and the Delhi homeboys.

For an hour, no one except the jaguar, took their eyes off Sandra. She captured our minds and we saw into the world of Lorca's bride. Toward the end of the performance she pulled a knife from underneath her blouse, danced and caressed its point, edge, width and length. She kissed the blade, she held it to her womb, to her breast, to her heart. She played with it like a fan and she recited the "Mother's Lament," the last words of Lorca's play:

> And it barely fits the hand
> but it slides in clean
> through the astonished flesh
> and stops there, at the place
> where trembles enmeshed
> the dark root of a scream.

The Delhi audience applauded and I went quickly to her side and took the knife. I realized then how dangerously sharp it was. Everyone acknowledged Lorca's greatness, praised Sandra's talent with an embrace. Sandra's performance in *Barrio* Delhi was one of the most eccentric experiences in my life.

But even more gratifying was opening night when *Barrio* Delhi politely invaded the Orange County Center. According to the subscribers of the Performer's Club, made up of Orange County's wealthy "ooh la las," the Orange County Center was the most beautiful structure in the county. The Delhi homeboys, encouraged by

Doña Rosina, declared a truce and invited other Orange County *barrios* to accompany them to Sandra's performance. Sandra had suddenly developed an unexpected following. Cars met at Centennial Park in Santa Ana and drove to Delhi to escort Sandra, chauffered in her Jaguar, to the theater. It was a sight that caught the attention of every pedestrian and car following the caravan. I estimated there were about three hundred low-riding cars cruising to the house of Orange County culture. The *Los Angeles Times* had estimated about two hundred "Chicano-painted and springy" automobiles. The *Orange County Register* declared there were "too many baroque-colored cruisers to count."

The Sandra Spear caravan arrived at the entrance and Sandra, Don Clemente without his jaguar, Doña Rosina, Keli and I alighted and entered. From each escorting car there came at least four or five people. For the first time in the history of the Orange County Center there was a capacity crowd of people from the Latino *barrios* coming to see a performance. If the *Los Angeles Times* was correct, there must have been close to two thousand folks who had come to spend a night at the theater. I walked proudly with Doña Rosina. We took our seats and enjoyed a captivating performance by Sandra Spear.

Sandra's parents were there. Phyllis' eyes confessed a mother's pride for Sandra's matchless performance. After the show Phyllis went backstage to embrace and kiss her. Bill stood by fidgeting, clearing his throat, obviously uncomfortable with Doña Rosina and the other people of Sandra's entourage. He was disgusted with their dress, posture and speech.

"Who are these people?" Bill asked.

"Our friends." I waited for his response.

"Friends, shit!"

The next morning the *Orange County Register* published a supportive review of "Blood Wedding," pointing out that the performance by Sandra Spear was exceptionally sensitive and meaningful to the unusual audience. It severely criticized the disrespectful attire of the people that came from Orange County's Hispanic community. "How can anyone enjoy a serious play sitting next to someone dressed like a hood?" asked the *Register's* reviewer. Later that week several letters to the editor expressed their concern and dismay as to "the disrespect the Hispanic community had toward the Theater. These/*barrio* homeboys, Mexican gangsters, looked absurd and defiant sitting in the architectural dignity of the Center. They should not have attended, if only to see one performing actress—Sandra Spear."

The *Los Angeles Times* was more generous. The reviewer enjoyed every "multivalent meaning of Lorca's metaphysical and mythological play." She went on to praise Sandra Spear as a "refreshing new actress whose political and social commitment are exemplary." The reviewer pointed out that, "The performance was great on stage as well as outside. The presentation of the young Hispanic adults from the different *barrios* was electrifying. Their clothes and cars were of the choicest homeboy fashion. They looked sharp and got along great. No need for the beefed-up security that came in later. The Hispanic theater-goers were some of Orange County's finest. It was a triumph for the Orange County Performance Center to have produced a great play, introduced a new star and attracted a substantial Hispanic audience."

Three nights after the play opened, the Center was filled to capacity with a large portion of Latinos in attendance. Every night Sandra had an escort. Two hours before curtain time low-rider cars from throughout the county began to cruise the area. There were no problems, everyone came, young and old, to see Lorca's tragic bride, played by Sandra Spear. However, the anti-Latino political forces in Orange County, ever fearful of being overrun and of losing their cultural spaces to the Mexicans, covertly convinced the theater administration that it was dangerous to allow such a large amount of *barrio* homeboys to gather in one place, and that the homeboys presence scared away the patrons.

The last performance of Lorca's "Blood Wedding" took place

six days after it opened. Sandra was not asked to leave, but from then on she was given only bit roles. The Center always cited its production of "Blood Wedding" as their outstanding example of community outreach and sensitivity to the Orange County Hispanic population. Yet the Center never again produced a play that remotely interested the *barrio* population, nor the Latinos living outside of the *barrios*. They continued to verbalize their interest and desire to respond to this audience, but they never acted. But Sandra made such an impact that other playhouses and theaters offered her many roles. Sandra always had work and she was happy.

10

She was happy even in the stone-cold afternoon which hid little knives that carved their way through her body as she wrote on my arms and back silent undecipherable words. My skin against hers. We kissed. I searched for water in her green-blue eyes and I found stone. Her breast, hips, thighs were sculptured marble; her mouth tasted of ash, and still I fell upon her body to quench my selfish passion. Sandra's words carved their way through my sexual mind. One by one they brought forth memories. She called my name, which I had forgotten at that instant when I undertook to split her in two. I moaned and she petted me like a puppy dog. She reassured me that she understood and that I had not failed her. There was nothing left of me now, only Sandra survived.

There was nothing left in me. I had forgotten the names of my friends. My world was Sandra, my work and our Delhi friends. I picked up my duffle bag and watched her sleep, coiled under the sheets, and she awoke startled. Her serpent eyes hissed.

"Are you going now?"

Above Orange County, above the smog barrier to the mountains, I retreated. She decided to stay home and study new offers, read new plays. For a weekend I wrote about us, about Sandra and me. There were moments when I attempted to reconstruct her face with words and the images they conjured up, but she turned into a mass of ash, the bride's knife in Lorca's play, a bag of visceral fluids, dry skin hanging from her emaciated bones, and she danced in a white gown at the bottom of a pit. She danced and danced until she melted away in a red sea leaving only her desperate green-blue eyes. I reached out to her as she struggled in the red whirlpool.

It was impossible to reach Sandra! Unhesitatingly, I let myself fall toward her, longing to return to life again.

I pursued other futures, other lives, others loves, but each led back to her to start again. I closed my eyes to reveal to myself where I had been, who I was, who she was, and why I desired her even now, why I loved her.

All night I made plans for us. We would take a trip. Sandra wanted to return to Mexico, to Yucatan and Guatemala, to explore the recently found archaeological sights. She once told me that anything that was found after a long time sustained for a moment intense magical waves. I laughed. These sights must possess super-magic waves, for they had been buried for more than a thousand years.

And we would go to Mexico City and stay at the María Cristina Hotel. Sandra described the room she wanted. To me, hotel rooms were all the same, but not for her. Each one that she remembered had a ritual, a way of entering, a way of allowing the room to let her share its space.

Sandra taught me rituals.

I blessed my car, my room, and when I finished writing, I blessed the pages which held the story of our time. Sandra had taught me to make them sacred. I thought I heard her voice. It was dawn, the sun broke through the dark thin line of night and began its dance slowly. I sat at the edge of the bed. Someone called my name. I must be sleeping, I thought, and fell face down on the bed. Moments later I was awakened by the weight of a gentle hand on my shoulder. Suddenly, I realized that the door was locked and no one could have entered. The hair on the nape of my neck chilled my back as fear immediately bolted me from the bed.

"*¡Híjole!* What is this?" I said.

Before me my grandfather Papá Damián greeted me.

I sat back on the bed, closed and opened my eyes. I heard his voice as I had heard it when I was a child. Long ago in Simons, in his room, in front of the *Virgen de Guadalupe*, after his death he had come to me.

"I have come to be your guide ... "

Curve after curve, I heard his voice, naming the streets and towns that we passed on the way down the mountain. Papá Damián thought he had lost me. We moved by faces in other cars, fourwheel drive vehicles, gas stations, houses, rooms, windows and doors. I rested at a park. There Papá Damián spoke to me again.

"Thank God I found you."

On the freeway, Papá Damián sang, talked about towns, streets, houses, rooms, a room in which Sandra waited.

"Slow down, slow down. You'll get there," I said to myself.

"Crap! What the hell is happening to me?"

I saw my car exit the Newport Freeway and drive toward Delhi.

11

It had been two days that Sandra slept and still felt weak. Large bruises covered her breasts, arms and thighs. She remembered a time when her blood did not batter her body. She remembered the women in the *plaza* of Oaxaca. They knitted, embroidered and wove chromatic blankets, *rebozos* and hats. Without hesitation she bought a hat. By the church, men read the newspaper and listened to the women and children sing. A strange melodic Indian language took over the *plaza*. Young men walked by and stared. She could almost feel their thoughts. Sandra liked their pristine odor of earth and semen. They inhaled her through their nostrils, mouth and eyes. Sandra imagined them as loving youth. It was as if everything was sacred.

Sandra stood at the center of the world. On the first night of existence, she chose an Indian. He traversed her with his broad face, black hair, brown joyful eyes. Toward the dawn of the first day they kissed and gave birth to the earth. Sandra was with him for several days and nights.

One morning Sandra and her lover walked to town. They passed the small jail where men and women maddened by *pulque* cursed their keepers. By the bank she remembered that she had to cash a traveler's check. Sandra passed the Indian huts and avoided a school of scorpions. Sandra's lover carefully picked two large ones and dangled them from their claws. He threw the creatures toward the Red Cross shed where a nun swept the herd off the porch. Finally, they arrived at Sandra's hotel and sat on the veranda overlooking the white ancient plaza. Sandra ordered fresh papaya, sweet bread and *café de olla*. She noticed that her elbows and

knees were swollen, but disregarded the soreness and related it to
her sudden hard lovemaking. No, she refused to allow the aches to
bother her. Sandra freely shared bread, alcohol, pot, the sun, her
body, her life. His smile became mine and she wondered where I
was the Sunday afternoon when she could hardly move her engorged
knees, ankles and elbows. Sandra's afflicted body, bruised by the
slightest confusion.

The morning after my departure, Sandra awoke with grossly
swollen ankles and hands. She lay still until ten, when she felt an
unbearable urge to spit. She struggled to the bath, and spit blood
into the wash bowl. With bloated stomach she sat on the toilet and
knew she was bleeding internally. Her clothes were at the foot of
the bed. As Sandra labored to put them on, a flow of blood came
from her nose. A strong chill oppressed her body. ... I will be
fine, Sandra thought, and refused to call the emergency number.

She shuffled to her car. Her pants were wet and smelled of
blood. Her white mask of terror, tethered above her moist crimson
blouse, frightened people. Several saw Sandra but were afraid to
approach. In that immense time she grew monstrous. She moved
into her slick Jaguar and drove toward Delhi.

"Oh, crap ... " Again a steady rush of blood issued from her
nose. She opened her mouth for oxygen. Sandra grabbed a handful
of tissue. In a second it was soaked. She grabbed my East Los
Angeles College sweat-shirt, held it to her nose, coughed heavily
and spit blood on the steering wheel. She was opening up all over.
She gasped for breath. She was almost there. She was confident
that they would help her, help her to die.

12

The Delhi homeboys had finished the garden and polished their cars while Keli dressed Doña Rosina's infected toe. With her good foot, Doña Rosina petted Don Clemente's jaguar. They spoke about the world and how fast things were changing. Suddenly, Sandra's Jaguar smashed into the fence and shattered their quiet Sunday afternoon.

The homeboys rushed to her side. They found her slumped against the window.

"*Dios mío*," Keli exclaimed as the homeboys carried Sandra to the porch.

"Here, wrap her in these!" Doña Rosina handed her sons several blankets.

"Put her in the back seat and take her to the hospital." Doña Rosina made her way to Sandra's car.

"Don Clemente, *llámale* a Flink . . . "

Escorted by five detailed, immaculately clean Delhi lowrider cars, a homeboy drove Doña Rosina, Keli and Sandra to the nearest hospital. The driver of Sandra's car floored the gas pedal every chance he had and arrived at the hospital in minutes. His homeboys followed close behind.

When the group carried Sandra into the emergency entrance, the nurse straightaway hit the security bottom.

"Stabbing victim in emergency, stat!"

Doña Rosina and Keli led the boys into a room with two empty examining tables. As they lay Sandra down, three security people entered and ordered the homeboys to place their hands on the table and spread eagle. They were searched for weapons. Two police officers appeared, initiated an aggressive interrogation while Sandra lay on the table, bleeding.

"Who stabbed her?" one cop asked.

"Where was she stabbed?" another pointed to Keli.

"Who was the other gang?" the cop yelled.

"*¿Dónde está el doctor?*" Doña Rosina called to the nurse.

"She's gonna bleed to death!" a homeboy pleaded.

"We have to fill out insurance forms before the doctor can see her," the nurse said.

"We don't have insurance! Call a doctor or she'll die!" screamed a homeboy into the face of one of the cops.

"Where did you steal the car?"

"It's hers," said Doña Rosina.

"You expect us to believe that your homegirl here owns a Jag?" said the cop.

The nurse chuckled, "And you don't have insurance."

"We don't, but maybe she does," said the homeboy driver.

"Send her to County, jail ward," the woman officer ordered. "All of you are going in!" yelled her partner.

"Fuck you! You're busting us for nothing." A homeboy moved toward the cop. "Let me give you something to throw me in jail for!"

At that point three more cops arrived and joined the circle of anger.

"The car checks out to a Sandra Spear," said one of the newly arrived cops.

"That's her!" Keli shouted in a shrill.

The woman cop stared down at Sandra. "She looks bad. Let's get her to County."

In spite of Doña Rosina's protests and offer to pay for the services, two orderlies placed Sandra on a cart and rolled her toward the exit. Two homeboys attempted to stop them, but the cops clubbed them down and took them away. Everyone was yelling as Sandra, ashen, was being moved to an awaiting ambulance.

A nurse with extremely short hair came in and grabbed one of the officers. "Take her back! She's hemophiliac. Flink and Revueltas have her covered." The nurse pushed Sandra back toward emergency.

"Set up for thrombin and blood transfusion, stat!" she called out to the first nurse.

Doña Rosina, Keli and the remaining homeboys followed behind the nurse. They stood against a wall and watched Flink and the short-haired nurse work rapidly. After twenty minutes Flink invited them outside.

"She is weak and will need blood. She's given her permission for a blood transfusion. All of you, except for Doña Rosina, must donate. Go home and bring people from the neighborhood. I hope she'll make it," Flink spoke softly. "Somebody leave a note for Dr. Revueltas."

"Hey, Flink, where's your assistant, the other *barrio* doctor? I'm glad you got here in time. Thank God you saved our ass. Tell mother *barrio* that her boys will be out tomorrow morning." The cop pointed to Flink and smiled goodbye.

13

Love had become a combat zone. We kissed and the world took
flight from where we undressed and held onto each other. Sandra's
body continued to bruise. The bleeding came frequently, but we
controlled it with infusions of thrombin, then with factor 8 powder
mixed in water. Sandra continued to work until one day the director
of the theatrical company asked her to take some time off to regain
her strength. She protested and claimed discrimination because of
her hemophiliac condition.

"Sandra, please understand, it's for your own good. Look at
yourself now, your arms and legs. You look as if you have been battered. You can't work like that!" The director ended the rehearsal
and walked off with his face as distorted as Sandra's. She remained
alone. It had been five months. She had lost weight and strength,
but not her desire.

"I'm a hemophiliac, but I can work!" Sandra screamed into the
empty theater.

She became disease-prone. She seemed never to be free of
viruses or bacteria. Flink and I performed more tests to find what
we suspected already. Sandra was a hemophiliac and suffered from
severe aplastic anemia, which caused her infections.

14

Bill and Phyllis arrived unannounced and threatened to take Sandra back home with them. When I entered our bedroom, Bill was packing bags while Phyllis was trying to convince her to return home. Phyllis insisted that new doctors, specialists in blood diseases, were what Sandra needed.

"No, mother, I'm staying. Gregory and Flink are doing everything they can," Sandra said, determined to remain.

I would not interfere. I would not keep her from her parents. I loved Sandra, but it had to be her decision to stay.

"Put those down, Dad! I'm staying here!"

Bill threw the luggage on the floor.

"Damn you! She would have been better off if she had never met you, Gregory. She'll die if she stays with you!" Bill left the room.

"But I'll die sooner at a sanitarium or at home! Don't you understand that being close to you makes me sadder? Don't you understand that when I see you, I remember the way it used to be? I can't bear your suffering. I have to try to live. I'll choose where I want to die."

At the door, Phyllis embraced me. "Anything. Money, whatever it takes. Call us," she said.

A buried groan came from Bill, as tears streamed down his face. "You brainwashed her."

15

At least once a week I visited my mother. I needed a break from Sandra. I rested, saw the world from a different place, from Español Street, the last remnant of Simons Brickyard. Yet even there she still pursued me. I became Sandra Spear-prone at every thought; every movement I related to her. To find a cure for Sandra became a medical compulsion, to write about her became a fetish. Being away from her allowed me to remember the beginning. I wrote and enjoyed recreating our life together. I returned with her to where it began. I searched for Sandra's face in the places we shared. I walked through my mind and found her journeying comfortably under an ageless sun. I was at her side as she was transfigured into a green-blue cypress and she spoke to me like a tree, a river, a seed. Suddenly she erupted and flew like a hummingbird, like a butterfly. Sandra laughed as she covered me with the sweet juice of an orange from my mother's orchard.

There in the house of my childhood, stronger then ever before, I felt impelled to write about us, to show every moment of our anguish and of our joy.

Strangely, when Flink solemnly came into the clinic with the results of the UCLA blood test, I was glad that at last we had identified exactly the disease that was devastating her. It had a name, but we were ignorant of what it meant.

Flink read carefully to himself, and finally with his prescribed "bad tidings" medical bearing he blurted out, "you have acquired immuno-deficiency syndrome, otherwise known as AIDS."

Her face tensed as if struck by a sharp pain.

"How could I have gotten that?" she said incredulously. "UCLA indicates that this disease might be transferred by contaminated blood," Flink said passively, still maintaining his medical formality.

"The transfusions!" I said, terrified for her.

"We gave her several. It was either the transfusions or she would have died." Flink faced Sandra. "You know that."

"What does it mean?"

Flink bit his lip. "It means you're sicker than before and it will probably get worse."

"How much . . . "

"I don't know. You do understand that very little is known about this disease. There is nothing for it. I'll call UCLA for more information. You also must understand that this disease is contagious. It's transmitted by semen and blood, possibly saliva."

A commotion interrupted from outside. Keli, Don Clemente and the homeboys carried a resistant Doña Rosina to the clinic. By the time she entered, her complaints had become quite audible.

"Finally, she's coming in," Sandra said with a chuckle.

"Yeah, now we have to operate," Flink said. "If we don't, she'll lose her foot from gangrene."

I had to stay. Sandra left, alone.

16

"No," I said. "We'll just have to deal with this."

I would not let go, even though Sandra had asked me to leave. For us the world had changed and our life became important. We did everything with more intensity and sensitivity to our surroundings. A walk in the park, lying in the grass and looking up at the sky, the stars at night, the smell of trees, the difference in light, the multitudes of silence, the variety of flavors of ice-cream, the distinct spaces, the difference in our bodies, the sound of our names. Only time passed as I watched her sleep. Only then was she at peace.

One night Sandra awoke terrified. She understood that even sleep attempted to forever deny peace. I made tea and we sat up discussing what she had seen. She spoke of it as real, but I believed the dream she described was prophecy; she had journeyed on a cart pulled by a powerful entity and she sat looking back from where she came. Sandra's journey was repeated interminably by a profusion of voices. In that place that she traveled, time was not as we knew it. As she spoke of this journey, I sensed that she had narrated this experience many times before. Advancing on this rough frustrating road, I saw myself watching her pass and always behind me there stood an older man.

"Your guardian angel . . . your guardian angel is always someone you loved," I said confidently.

"I wonder who'll be mine?" she asked and sipped her tea.

Although her dream was real, there was a confidence and warmth about Sandra gained from this knowledge that she began to possess. In her eyes there danced flame, her ears heard a careful passion, her lips tasted of soft sweet ash, her fearful tongue and touch caressed my thoughts. From that ardor of desire, Sandra began to burn on the surface of her body. She had not noticed, nor felt it yet, but on the underside of her forearm grew a reddish blotch.

17

A month later, when Sandra went to talk to the program director at the Orange County Theater, she had three burn areas on her arm, several on her hands, one large new sarcoma on her neck and one developing on her right cheek under her ear. She went to him to discuss scripts that she had read months ago and characters that fascinated her, that she wanted to play. She hadn't felt weak for some time, she felt positive and wanted to work.

Although Sandra knew the director's secretary well, the woman was cautiously formal and immediately asked her to take the furthest chair. She hurried into the director's office and soon emerged and grabbed her purse, all the while regarding Sandra as an unpredictable, contaminated animal. Without saying a word, the secretary ran out of the reception area.

Sandra had been warned about suspicions, that people would take them as true. She expected that some people would not want to deal with her, but not to even be in the same room—this was a little drastic. She stood up when the director appeared at the doorway of his office.

"No, please, sit right down. I know you've been ill. Please stay right where you are."

The "please" sounded more like a warning than a gesture of courtesy.

"What did you want to see me about?" he asked maintaining his distance.

Sandra handed him the plays and said, "Well, I came about auditioning for these parts."

He pushed his hands palms-up toward her. "No, it's okay, you keep them." He continued, "Yes, I'm sure you would do an excellent job, but as of this moment, no appointments for auditions are being made."

"Don't give me that! There are people on stage at this very moment reading," Sandra said.

The director took one step back into his office. "Sandra, I know, but there are rumors circulating."

"Rumors?"

"Forgive me for being blunt. But many people believe you have AIDS and will not work with you."

As Sandra started for the door, the director moved back into his office and prepared to close it.

"And that includes you."

Half-hidden, the director called out, "You just don't know about this sickness. Nobody wants to endanger their lives by working with you." He closed the door.

As she departed, seven people were waiting outside. They talked quietly.

"AIDS," someone whispered.

Sandra had to walk about five feet from them; as she approached, they moved even further.

"She has what?" were the last words she heard.

Sandra was transmuted into a decomposing creature, bursting with foul-smelling miasma, spilling fluids and dropping maggots in its wake, and decorated with a crown of filthy flies.

18

Time for me became more demanding. I had to work for Flink. He depended on me, the people who came to the clinic needed me. But I wanted to spend more time with Sandra. I needed to be there when she called for help, when she awoke at night, frightened. She refused to see her parents. But they would come late at night when she slept. Bill and Phyllis were resigned. My staying with Sandra made Bill less angry, but still he blamed me for what had happened to her.

My visits with Mother became a necessity. I looked forward to driving early Friday mornings on the Santa Ana Freeway, leaving everything behind, traveling thirty-three miles north into another world. I enjoyed sitting with her for breakfast, then taking flowers to Father at Rose Hills Cemetery. My time with Mother became a time of writing and listening. I wrote about Sandra and me and listened to Mother's past. Mother seemed to be slipping back, constantly remembering Father, their life together, my brothers and sisters, when our house in Simons had burned down, the building of the new house, what a crazy boy I was . . .

Mother always remembered.

Friday mornings with Mother brought our lives into a better perspective. My staying and caring for Sandra was natural. There was no need to feel guilty.

"Octavio, when was life really ours?" Mother asked after placing a bouquet of flowers on Father's tomb.

She was correct. It was never ours. We were not who we were, in the past, in the present, in the future. Our life, ourselves, belonged to others and those others belonged to us. I was someone else when I

110

was myself. Fearfully, I searched for myself in my patients, friends, those whom I loved. Curiously, life was somewhere else, never in the place where I acted; life was always further away, outside me, from me, but never in my control. My face was Sandra's face. My lonely collective face was everyone's face.

Once I dozed off on the couch. Mother stood before me. She spoke, but what her words whispered were images which revealed her other forms. Around her danced life and death. She was virgin of the sun and moon, water and earth, fire and wind. Since birth I had been falling toward her who pushed me out to life. I yearned for her to prevent my fall and to push me out to life once more. On me she tossed seeds of corn and her hand gently pushed my hair away from my forehead.

"*M'ijo*, it's getting late and the freeway will be terrible if you delay."

19

Sandra had overcome her first bout with PCP, pneumocystis carinii pneumonia, and waited for the next opportunistic infection to attack. In her mind antibiotics were the chemicals that had cured the PCP. She was convinced that she should take them daily for preventive purposes. Flink and I refused to dispense the drugs that Bill and Phyllis had recommended.

"These drugs are illegal in the US," Flink said.

"You want me to die!" Sandra screamed hysterically.

"Scream, get it all out," I said and listened to her sobbing.

I knew how they had treated Sandra at the UCLA clinic. Several doctors and nurses absolutely refused to be in the same room with her. The doctors that treated the pneumonia talked to her by phone or through me. They considered Sandra a human scourge, a Pandora's box filled with diseases capable of destroying humanity. Sandra was simply a research case, a human disease puzzle to be solved. The endocrinologist and the hematologist saw her as a job risk. Their complaint was that they did not get combat pay for endangering their lives with scum like her. I don't believe any were sympathetic.

Once I took a waste basket filled with tissue paper that Sandra had used and placed it out in the hall to remind them to take it. When the nurses saw what I had done, they belligerently forced me to take the wastebasket back to the room and to wait for the janitor. The janitors never came and her room was transformed into a waste bin. She remained in the hospital for almost three weeks. Her condition got better, then deteriorated, then stabilized. Sandra's health was a rollercoaster ride to the ends of the world, until the end of her existence here on earth. Yet she maintained confidence that she would be renewed.

The day that Flink refused Sandra the drugs, he also did not touch her. He maintained his distance. He revealed his fear and intention of not treating her further.

"I can't do anything more for you. I can't give you those drugs. My hands are tied. You must seek help somewhere else!" Flink was definite. "Furthermore, there are patients who have stopped coming to the clinic because they are afraid to run into you. I'm sorry, but I have to tell you the truth." Flink gave me the syringe. I did the blood work and injected the drugs.

The night before, there had been a blizzard in the mountains, even Saddleback Mountain had a foot of snow. It was a cool February day. We sat on the apartment balcony contemplating the serene white mountains. Sandra was noticeably tired. Her arms were bruised more than usual. She had contracted another cold. She had lost twenty pounds, down to exactly ninety pounds. Her body contrasted with the white mountains, but her strength and endurance were as great.

"Gregory, I need to go to Mexico. We must go to the places of power that Doña Rosina has described," Sandra said in deep voice.

In two days I made arrangements. Bill thought we were mad. Phyllis gave us money which Sandra refused, but I accepted. Flink gave us a two-week supply of necessary medications. Doña Rosina informed us of the places we were to go to seek help.

On the eve of our departure, Bill and Phyllis and my Mother met for the first time. That night, Flink, Doña Rosina, Don Clemente, Keli and the homeboys came to say goodbye. Present for only a short while was Papá Damián, whom I had not seen for some time, but on that day he appeared standing behind my Mother. Our old folks possessed a kind of magic, a relationship to the past that they carried in their minds and faces. His presence, more than anything else, was the sign that convinced me that our venture was correct. Papá Damián, I was sure, would be our guide.

We had a party. There was a wedding atmosphere, a celebration
before the honeymoon. Keli had made a *Feliz Viaje* cake which
Sandra and I cut. We fed each other the first slices. Bill took
photographs.

From the excitement and emotion, Sandra had a severe nose
bleed, but we stopped it fairly quickly. Flink warned her about the
plane and the altitude of Mexico City.

"I won't bleed," she declared defiantly.

On a clear morning our parents and Delhi friends escorted us
to the airport. In the belly of a metal bird we rose above those
white mountains, above the sea and banked southward. In about
three and half hours we looked down into a volcanic cradle crowned
by Popocatepetl and Ixtacoatepetl, two white magical peaks, the
symbols of a legendary love affair and the eternal natural sentinels
of Tenochtitlan.

20

Enchanted by the city, we eagerly allowed our minds to be invaded by a kind of collective hypnosis. A reverie brought about by a continuous differentiation of the old and the new, and the rich and the poor, and the faces of people who represented nomadic Mesoamerican, European, African and Asian cultures. These were the Mexicans, inheritors of the world's cultural tribes.

For the trip Sandra had draped her ninety-pound body in faded jeans, an 'LA Rams' sweat shirt, tennis shoes, a blue baseball cap and black sun glasses. The cab driver hurried to carry our duffel bags.

"I help *la niña*," he said.

He had put the bags at the entrance of the María Cristina Hotel and there I took a photo of Sandra and the driver pointing inadvertently to the marble French foyer—one of thousands of artistic treasures taken for granted in Mexico City. We rested for an hour, then went down to the garden for a drink. Across the way, Papá Damián, sitting alone in a white wrought-iron chair, wrote about us. She was oblivious of him.

In our room after dinner, I called Doña Rosina's friend, Señora Jane Krauze. Señora Jane had expressed her pleasure to receive us at the women's retreat in the city of Tepotzotlan. The very next morning, precisely at ten, as she had indicated, a car arrived. After a restful night, Sandra seemed to enjoy the trip through the city and its outskirts. Her face cleansed by slumber, her eyes sparkled with curiosity. Our trip passed in silence as we began to climb above the Mexico City suburbs.

We asked several questions, but the woman driver never responded. Sandra nudged her shoulders and stopped asking questions for fear of seeming impolite.

"She can't speak," Sandra whispered.

The woman driver stopped in the plaza before the intricately carved massive doors of the portal of the Jesuit Seminary which was the heart of the city. She led us to the entrance of the museum. There was a small bookstore, with histories of Mexico, the Jesuits, the Indians and of the seminary of Tepotzotlan. An older man in a blue uniform pointed to a woman who handed me two tickets from under an oblique plastic window. I slipped a hundred peso bill under the opening and got forty back.

The woman led us deliberately through high white-washed corridors of small cells. She stopped at each one where inside a display of furniture, of life in the eighteenth century was contained. My mind's eye, the scent of the old stone walls and wooden floors, and the geometry of the architecture told me that I had been here before. An absurd thought, but yet a strong and strangely comforting one. Finally we stopped at the end of a corridor under a vaulted cupola, before a carved stairway. A small brass sign read *Biblioteca Religiosa*.

The immense library was a treasure of leather-bound books from the eighteenth and nineteenth centuries. A carved reading table, two gold lamps, comfortable chairs and a small round tea table decorated the room.

"Beautiful," Sandra said.

We had been alone for at least a half hour, browsing through the books, when our chauffer silently placed tea and bread on the table.

"Why are we here? *¿Dónde está la señora Jane?*" Sandra asked the woman.

The chauffer seemed startled, yet she gestured with her fingers that it would be a little longer. She poured the tea and left us.

"Sandra, this whole section is books describing Indian

medicine," I said excitedly.

Sandra handed me a journal. "And personal journals written by Spanish doctors who lived centuries ago."

The door opened and a young woman entered, dressed in what appeared to be an expensively tailored navy blue business suit. Tall, with curly black hair, she offered her hand genuinely. We felt reassured and confident that she had accepted us, that she knew about Sandra's illness and that in some strange way, perhaps, she would be able to help. As she spoke we knew that this was Señora Jane. From her motion, her speech, her sight, her fragrance there emanated a strong positive force. She naturally commanded our attention.

"Life is a gift and worth living," she said to Sandra. "I am a librarian," she said and took the journal that I held. "This journal was written by your *tocayo*," she smiled.

"His what?" Sandra asked.

"A person with the same first name," Señora Jane said and placed the journal back on the shelf. "The Gregory of this journal was a man who also dealt with devastating illness."

Señora Jane was a woman who seemed to be out of place in this ancient seminary. She had saved and studied thousands of volumes which at one time had been marked for destruction by the Catholic hierarchy. There was no doubt in my mind that she commanded their knowledge.

She walked us through the ancient gardens and paths of the seminary. Sandra and I pulled the weeds growing around the grave markers and read names such as Jude, Marisela, Mónica Marisela and my *tocayo*, Gregorio. She took us through a house that was said to be haunted by the souls of those buried in the cemetery. At the center of the house, Señora Jane explained, "the Indians say that this is holy ground, for thousands of people were cured here by the spirits that are buried in the church yard."

"Do you believe that?" Sandra asked.

"You should," she said.

I watched the grave stones which were now being cleaned by Papá Damián. He confirmed my madness. Señora Jane laughed and waved toward the church-yard graves.

21

Sandra awoke. I heard her labor to swallow. A dry deep cough told of her pain and swollen throat. I reached for the light and found her sitting up with a glass of water in hand. Drenched in sweat, she shook from icy chills. She handed me the glass and we both observed the enlarged purplish lumps beneath the skin of her arms. Sandra screamed. I embraced her. Two women with a bowl of water and towels came into our room. They took Sandra from me and calmed her.

That night I saw terror in her eyes.

Señora Jane explained that what Sandra had felt was the first grasp of death on her being.

"Don't fear it. You must learn to accept that seizure. It will come more often. Soon you will learn to talk to that shape. It will constantly be with you, right up to your transmutation. All people fear that moment. We see it as a modification. Your body is changing rapidly now. Understand your opportunity. We are happy for you. You bring joy to those who love you. You must be proud. Do not be ashamed of your decaying body. Decay is a natural process. God and the energies of the earth are calling you to join them in their metamorphosis of all of us. I love you. I love your decay. I love your illness. I will marry you and love you to the last day. I will hold you in your putrefaction. I am your ally up to the gates through which someday all humanity will be privileged to pass. I will guide you, bathe you, clean your open sores, comfort your pain, clean your excrement, dry your urine, endure your odor, lie down with you, laugh with you, be happy with you." Señora Jane and I prayed until daybreak.

For seven days we had been her guest at her Rancho de la
Sonrisa Solar. Papá Damián prayed to a painting of the *Virgen de
Guadalupe*. He pointed to a bag which contained Sandra's medica-
tion.

"Give it to her now," Señora Jane said.

"But this is not her ... " I stammered.

Papá Damián encouraged Sandra to take the medication. Sandra was over me. She whispered that she was not afraid and ingested
the odd substance from the leather pouch.

"This is Nahaultzin's nourishment," Señora Jane said. Time
lost, we awoke Sunday morning to the sounds of young women
chatting. It was visiting day at the Rancho de la Sonrisa Solar, where
the rich of Mexico City sent their daughters who had demonstrated
in their actions a tinge of dangerous proclivities. Here they were
reeducated, cleansed of those propensities.

The ranch house was an old hacienda converted into dormitories, classrooms, clinic and theater. Señora Jane and several
Carmelite nuns administered the school. Sandra and I walked the
grounds that day. She felt wonderful. She wore a long white skirt
and a long sleeve blouse. They covered the open sores on her
deformed limbs. The dark glasses hid her swollen eyelids. She
walked with her mouth open; for the mucous membranes in her
nasal passages hindered her breathing. Her enlarged tongue and
distended lips slurred her speech. A baritone laughter called attention to her. From where we sat, we saw the families arriving to visit
their daughters.

"How do you feel today?" I asked.

"Strange, this place, I mean," Sandra whispered. "Strong, I
feel strong."

"Tomorrow we leave," I said. "Señora Jane will take us to
Tepotzotlan. Sandra, you will grow even stronger there."

That night she slept soundly, perhaps her deepest slumber. I
listened to the pleurisy in her lungs, to the thick phlegm in her throat
and waited, alert, in case she needed me. Helpless, I could only

make her comfortable on her voyage. The last image I remembered was Papá Damián tending to Sandra and praying to the *Virgen de Guadalupe*, who flew on a fiery crest above her.

22

We spent several days exploring the countryside surrounding the ancient town of Tepotzotlan. The Indians offered their homes and we joined in the celebration of the energy of Tepoztecatl, the rustic god of the harvest and strong drink. Accompanied by Señora Jane and her mute driver, we ate and drank in honor of the local god of Tepotzotlan. At night we observed the making of the fires encircling the sacred pyramid and joined in the rituals played out in the temple.

In those moments of joy I forgot about Sandra's illness. I searched for her in the crowd of dark faces. She danced, she drank the liquors prepared for her. Yet, she was never intoxicated. She seemed happy and strong. The *curanderas* tended to her. They taught her about herbs and plants to ease her pain. The *curanderas* were not afraid of Papá Damián, who worked among them, and they were not afraid of Sandra's illness. They gave it a strange name, *La Mona*.

"It is an ancient plague. There are records describing it. It is a disease that makes you look like a clown with black rings round your eyes, bruised, deformed arms and a white speckled tongue. Your limbs become weakened to the point where they are like the arms of a raggedy doll," Señora Jane interpreted the *nahuatl* narrative of the *curandera* who examined Sandra's body.

The *curandera*, dressed in flamboyant crimson colors, her face painted like a whore, was not what I expected. She felt, heard, smelled and scrutinized Sandra's physique as if handling a puzzle of flesh. Her gesticulations, body gestures and tone of voice were sincere and humorous. She was funny. We laughed. All three of us: Sandra, Señora Jane and me. Señora Jane continued her simultaneous interpretation.

"There is no cure for *La Mona*. We can delay the natural progress of your life cycle by simple amputation." The painted-face woman giggled and patted Sandra's knee. "Although I laugh, I do not jest," the garish scarlet *curandera* spoke in an ironically sensual manner. "Remember, you are not dying. You are experiencing a radical change accompanied by terror and pain. Now you must learn to counter those forces with laughter. Learn to laugh again. That is what you need most at this time, learn to laugh again." The *curandera* sat back on her haunches.

"She has finished," Señora Jane said.

"Please, ask how we can pay her?" Sandra said.

Señora Jane asked.

"You are a special child, a special source of energy. You have honored and blessed me, and I wish that the world outside the sacred triangle of Tepotzotlan will honor and respect you to the end of your journey." The *curandera* took Señora Jane's hand and thanked her. She embraced Sandra and kissed her forehead. Papá Damián witnessed the complete examination. He led the way out of the sacred hut.

Outside under a star-flooded sky, the eyes of a people who had lived before and who had walked these Mexican paths accompanied us through the bright night to our room in the Dominican Monastery of Natividad de Nuestra Señora. The brightness of the night revealed a row of Crosses of Alcántara, the Dominican insignia, deeply sculptured in the stone walls of the gallery that led to the long corridor to our room. The starlight transformed them into rows of dark shadows, like the purple tumors strung down Sandra's arms, wrapped around her legs and splattered on her back. Upon passing the threshold of our room, Sandra collapsed. I undressed her, pulling her blouse away from the open boils on her body. She did not feel the pain, only the horror. She had lost more weight. A thin layer of skin covered her spine. Her shoulder blades and

arms were like the wings of prehistoric birds. Her ribs were like
iron grates. Sandra shivered from fever and begged for warmth as
I injected her with vinblastine.

"We should try another treatment," I said.

Kaposi's Sarcoma ravaged her body. Moritz Kaposi described
what I treated as idiopathic, multiple pigmented sarcomas of the skin
in 1872, and then someone decided it should be named after him.
What a way to be remembered. I don't think he liked the suggestion.
He preferred sarcoma idiopathicum multiplex hemorrhagicum. I
recalled reading this in a class on rare diseases. Nothing could help
us now. KS wasted no time nor opportunity to attack her.

"We need to go back home," I said. "If we don't, you will get
worse."

"You can't save me. But perhaps they can."

Sandra looked out toward the towering mountains not far from
Cuernavaca. I left the windows open for her to see the mountains
and countryside illuminated by stars. Strangely, for an instant, out
of the sky there fell a multitude of lightning bolts. "Did you see
them?" I asked.

"Yes," Sandra said in a voice that was not hers.

23

Señora Jane and several Indian men and women *curanderos* came in the late afternoon to offer prayers, medicines and laughter to Sandra Spear. Stately and proud folk, they moved about politely and confirmed great respect for their patient. Sandra graciously accepted all gifts and joined in the laughter. There was never a dull moment. We ate and drank *pulque* and gave homage to Tepoztecatl.

The sun sunk to places beyond our sight. Señora Jane and the *curanderos* examined Sandra. They brought water and washed her ulcerated lesions. They dressed her in clothes which were many colored and expressed the Indian and modern dress. Her dress was transcultural, transhistorical. She was a comet radiating a throng of flaming tails. Surrounded by Indians who touched her in a sacred way, who sang mystic incantations, who moved around her escorting her to the *posa*, a vault with two semicircular arched entrances with quasi-Ionic half columns supporting the arches. At each corner, high enough for people to reach were shell-headed niches with vases filled with flowers. Crosses of Alcántara decorated the columns below the white capitals. I stood outside before the archway. The mountains rose above and merged the Dominican and Indian *posa* into one configuration.

The *posa* was built directly over a sacred point of the earth, an apex of a cosmic pyramid constructed by the energies, the gods of the cosmos. The three points of one side of the pyramid were constituted by the mountains, the monastery and the town. Here in this triangle, the gods of the cosmos rested during their internal journey through the time and space of infinity. With the gods' presence, great natural energies amassed and all the logic of existence as known to humanity was eradicated for a moment. During this period the alien, unaccountable, miraculous might occur. Señora Jane's thoughts floated near, but never next to me. I heard, but never saw her. Night fell onto the sacred apex and the incantations grew stronger as more people joined in the ritual. Sandra danced like energy among them. Serpents wreathed out from her punctured skin. Sandra was the god Coatlicue and I feared her.

A frenzy of music and chants engulfed the *posa*. Hundreds of people sang. Sandra grew stronger as the ceremony progressed. She danced faster, sang louder and embraced the Indian men and women who came near her. In the early morning, when the sky became white, there arrived a sacred drink and ancient stones of fire. Señora Jane and a *curandera* pulled from a leather bag twenty-five luminous rocks from the heavens. The stones were placed in a heated caldron in the middle of the *posa*.

"Drink this potion and swallow these stones of life," Señora Jane offered.

A potent radiance flowed from Sandra. Scabs fell as the ulcers burned away. There was no more pain for her. The light of the sky became a sea of percussion and melodies in which Sandra and I navigated.

24

The homeboys wore their "Guadalupe" jackets. Since we returned their number had multiplied. Doña Rosina counseled them to continue school and to restrain from fighting. They were always present. They made up Sandra's royal guard. They were her eyes toward the future and they gave her strength. She wanted a homeboy posted twenty-four hours at her door. They loved her when she was well and they loved her now at a high point of deterioration.

Doña Rosina suggested that Sandra stay. Keli was able to tend to her. Keli started nurse's training with Flink, who supplied the needed medication. I held her arm as Keli inserted the syringe for the last intravenous injection of Trimethoprim-sulfamethoxazole. The PC pneumonia rapidly deprived Sandra's body of oxygen. She labored for each mouthful of air.

"*Aquí tienes más agua, hijo,*" my mother said.

My mother placed a bowl of water and towels at Sandra's side. I gave her water. I ran the cool towel over her forehead and under her neck. I cooled her seared emaciated body that gave forth a sea of salty water.

My mother had been with Doña Rosina shortly after our return. During that time Papá Damián appeared to watch over us. Sandra's parents offered their house, but Sandra refused. She did not want to fill the house with the odor of her condition, with the living visions of her body, with her pulsating painful ache.

"Mom and Dad, remember me the way I was."

Sandra denied them access to her room. She did not want to see them. But when she was in the morphine induced ghost-sleep, beneath a blue heavy sea, they came and sat by their only daughter.

127

She had become their child again. Bill and Phyllis faithfully bathed and changed her clothes. They slept at her side, held and kissed her. When Sandra slept they were always there.

Flink came often. He saw Sandra once and after that he never came into her room. His reaction did not surprise me. What her body was today he saw once before as a child. He was afraid of her more now than the day he described her illness. He was afraid to see her, afraid of the memories brought back by the sight of her. He always left what we needed on the kitchen table.

Don Clemente and his jaguar kept guard, sitting with Doña Rosina on the porch of the small white house in Delhi. He was the only one of us who admitted that he kept guard against Death. He declared that he and his jaguar could see *La Calaca* coming. At times I wondered if he felt Papá Damián, who often accompanied him in his vigilance. He waited day and night on the porch. No matter what we said, he refused to leave.

"*Aquí tienes más agua, hijo,*" my mother said.

Sandra pushed the towel away and it became a sponge of memories. Objects that she touched became filled with her. The last sweater worn by her still lay across a chair. Yesterday, she thumbed through a family photo album, which I later hid. She signed legal documents prepared by Bill and Phyllis. I saved the black fountain pen and the last pencil she wrote with. Her clothes hung in the closet, her slippers waited faithfully under the bed.

The white wall of the room which Sandra attempted to clean with a wet tissue, and on which she hung pictures for Doña Rosina, saved the memory of her desire to be useful up to the last moments of her life. She struggled now to breathe. She opened her eyes once. Sandra pointed to the door.

"Your mother and father, everybody is here with you, Sandra. Do you want to see them?"

With great effort Sandra nodded a clear approval. In less than a minute we surrounded her bed. Her mother and father held her hands.

While I looked upon the faces that cared for Sandra, she gently expired. She, Sandra, who entered, changed and loved my life exactly as I loved hers, who called from deep within my soul an ancient tear that would forever taste to me like our love, the tear both of us shared at that final moment of her passage.

Book Three

LAMEX

Based on Southwestern architectural designs and constructed with mid-twentieth century adobe clay, the house has stood for ninety-nine years on high ground. The adobe structure has approximately four thousand square feet of living area with a large living, family and dining rooms, four bedrooms, a combination den and library and a spacious kitchen.

It was built as my grandparent's dream house. A three-hundred-and-sixty-degree view of the surrounding mountains and the Hemet Valley are part of the package. Grandfather Gregory planted a variety of fruits on the acreage. He built an outside workshop and a small barn for a few horses, goats and chickens. He named his twenty-acre parcel El Rancho de los Revueltas. Today, the ranch is one of the exclusive Oakridge Ranches in the Higher Life Existence city of Temecula. The well pumps precious clean water. From where in the bowels of the terrified earth the crystal clear liquid comes, only God knows.

Nearby San Gorgonio and San Jacinto, two pine covered peaks, rise above the estate where grandfather Gregory spent his last years. I have lived in this house for fifteen years. From the library, I view the city of Hemet below in the hot flatlands. Earlier today, dozens of buses with fourth-life people toured through the Oakridge Ranch Estates and headed down the mountain to attend the performance of *Ramona*, a play that depicts Indian, Mexican and Spanish cultures two hundred years ago in the region. The Higher Life Existence city of Temecula is situated northeast of San Diego and southeast of Los Angeles, California. The house is only minutes from two computer travelways that run from Los Angeles to Mexico City. One follows the Pacific Coast and the other travels through the desert, right through the center of Mexico directly to its heart, ancient Tenochtitlan, the name under which the Aztecs ruled nearly six hundred years ago, today Mexico City, the capital. The region from the center of Mexico to the Pacific Coast is known as the Lamex Coastal Region of the Triple Alliance. The Lamex Coastal Region is also the Lamex Health Corridor of the Triple Alliance, of which I am the Medical Director. My particular specialty is medical-biological environmental genetics, a long title for a simple doctor of gene engineering. I have had this job for as long as I have lived in the house. My first assignment with the LHC was at the Newport Center for Health Maintenance.

After graduating from medical school and in the seventh month of a nine-month crash program in medicine and language at the University of Mexico, Mexico City, I sent resumes to areas where I wanted to work and live, anywhere in Southern and Baja California, preferably. During the eighth month, while I researched severe pulmonary cases in Mexico City, a Mikros Lilianov sent me an invitation via computer to present my investigations to the LHC board of directors. Although I had a hunch, I never allowed myself to think that my first choice was even a remote possibility. That evening at dinner, Mikros Lilianov offered me an entry-level medical position with LHC, a first job that doctors only dream about.

Getting the post at Newport Health, a health center that served a Higher Life Existence Concentration, was an exaggeration of luck.

Pleased, I returned to Mexico City to find to my great surprise a job offer waiting there as well. These events of good fortune gradually developed strong positive sensory communication pressures indicating to me that I had no choice, that the events had planned in themselves there own occurrence, that they had recognized that our coming together in a precise time and place was symmetrically correct.

After three years, the directorate assigned me to the main research center of the Lamex Health Corridor in Los Angeles and

Mexico City. Straightaway, I was able to assist the director in several spontaneous health emergencies that occurred in both Los Angeles and Mexico City. One week after my superior performance under crisis conditions was recognized, I was appointed to the director's position. I simply worked to my utmost capacity, unaware that my boss was under severe criticism. Without fail, when I received an emergency designation, I thought of him. He was a constant reminder of a man who had failed because of lack of preparation.

I thought of him as I observed Gabriela "Gabi" Chung drive our medical crisis vehicle up to the house. Shortly, we would program into one of the computer travelways and head south to San Diego, where an unknown contaminant had invaded a small Lower Life neighborhood and caused the death of five hundred people in a few hours. I had ordered several mobile medical units to the scene, but they had not found the cause or the antidote. The units in San Diego described horrible physical deterioration and completely foreign symptoms. Gabi maneuvered the emergency vehicle up to the front gate. She pushed the door open.

"Hurry up, Gregory. The death rate has accelerated," she said, as she smiled surrounded by thousands of colorful computer lights that flashed softly onto her Asian face. My personal guide and assistant in work and in life (there was no difference) was Gabi Chung. She had assisted the preceding three directors and had worked on some of the worst natural disasters in recent times. She had completed her medical work in South America and had done graduate studies in genetics at the Mexico City research center. She piloted our emergency vehicle into the entry position on the computer travelway. She punched in our code and destination and in thirty seconds, just enough time to prepare psychologically, our vehicle was catapulted into the supersonic travelway. We both re-laxed and studied the latest reports that came from the stricken area. I glanced over at Gabi and watched her couple her robotic right arm into the electrical charger. Upon entering the car I had noticed the smell of burning flesh—a sure sign that she needed to recharge the arm. Just one of the inconveniences of severing an arm and hand from the elbow and replacing it with a computerized knowledge bank whose fingertips were laser surgical instruments and knowledge cylinders.

The Directorate no longer considered Gabi an experiment. She was one of a hundred who five years ago had signed on to the successful medical robotics program. The Directorate sent me a letter of invitation to participate in the program and gave me one year to decide. I understood I didn't have much of a choice. The competition to accumulate knowledge into one brain and one body for immediate access had escalated for fifty years, since the world had turned against humanity.

Gabi pulled her hand away and rested. "That sure felt good," she said.

"It smells better," I replied, smiling.

Pre-arrival yellow signals went on. In a matter of minutes we would step out into an area devastated by a spontaneous plague. Silently, I prayed for God's help and that the computerized ghosts of my ancestors would accompany me in this battle.

For many years I have been frequented by two individuals, Papá Damián and Grandfather Gregory. It is comforting to know that they come when I most need them. They are individual human lives who have escaped the parameters of time and the limitations of the computers that house the detailed descriptions of history. Computer ghosts are not uncommon; but usually they are not as strong as these two colleagues of mine. The yellow light flashed rapidly. In seconds we would disembark.

2

As we approached the Lower Life Existence concentration, Gabi and I discussed a plan of research, identification and eradication of the germ or poison that had killed hundreds of Lower Life citizens. The city had an ironic name, Chula Vista, or beautiful view in English. Although Chula Vista was a small LLE city, it took longer to get to the center than what we had calculated. The road spiraled down and finally up to a high plateau where the lights from the ocean flickered through the late afternoon grey hue. Up here on high ground, we stood before the electrical wire-fenced medical facilities, where the ill had been isolated. Every ten minutes, helicopters brought in more casualties.

From what I understood, the sum of these LLE cities had the same history. Built around old prison facilities, most of the population consisted of the Lumpen, the criminals and dregs of our society. The failure of our nation's penitentiaries to rehabilitate people had created a one hundred percent recidivism. No matter the sentence, it was understood to be life in a penal colony. The prisoners made the best out of a bad situation and encouraged their families to settle down outside the prison. Prison towns sprang up around the isolated penitentiaries. After ten years of bloody riots and just before the formation of the Triple Alliance, our country designated the prisons as self-governing LLEs. People found guilty of antisocial behavior that required separation from society were condemned to one of the nation's LLEs.

With a population of three hundred thousand, Chula Vista, near what used to be the international boarder between Mexico and the United States, was one of the smaller LLEs in the country.

Gabi and I walked inside the central compound and listened to the report of the medical unit leader. "Can't locate the source," the medical leader yelled over the incoming helicopters. "They just fade away!"

Gabi calmed the leader, whose voice gave away his nervousness and fear as he attempted to describe the rapid deterioration of the victims. Helicopters were coming in faster now.

"Let's take a look," Gabi suggested.

We entered a large, two-level dormitory. Victims leaned against bars and walls, sprawled on the floor and huddled under furniture as if seeking the darkness of the womb. The eyes of the poisoned bulged from their faces.

A woman reached out to us. She extended a grotesquely bruised hand. Her feet and legs appeared battered. To the touch, her limbs felt like balloons filled with liquid. The woman rolled to the side, made an effort to push herself up with her hands, which burst and discharged a fetid substance. The woman collapsed.

Gabi extended her computerized arm, extracted a scalpel and cut a sliver of tissue from the woman's infected hand. With a syringe, she siphoned yellowish liquid from the woman's forearm. She retracted both instruments.

"In five minutes I'll have the results," she said proudly. She walked off to talk to other victims.

I called after her. "Gabi, stay close by, I want to know the results as soon as possible."

The hundreds of people crowded into that dormitory suffered silently. Not one cry did I hear. The helicopters had stopped coming. Perhaps the plague had subsided and moved away to another place or time. Totally unpredictable, these spontaneous plagues could appear anywhere. Produced by humanity's harvest of waste, they traveled through the air, land and sea and penetrated populated areas, sometimes killing thousands. Scientist throughout the world had identified thousands of these living cancers of the earth. They were of all sizes, colors and smells. Some were invisible. From our pollution we had created energy masses that destroyed or deformed everything in their path.

Born in the depths of the Pacific Ocean about one hundred miles offshore, three huge masses of filth had developed organically and begun to move of their own accord. The Triple Alliance ships circled the energy masses, keeping them stationary. If these masses of living waste were to throw themselves onto the coastal shores, there would be an unavoidable catastrophe.

I turned away from a child whose reddish-colored extremities had begun to turn black and blue. In those innocent blue eyes the clean sea appeared as it was hundreds of years ago. I leaned him back against his dead mother. I suppose I should have felt sorrow, but that was an emotion that humanity had done away with long ago. I stood up to see Gabi point to a small rectangular screen on her computer arm.

"Plutonium oxide, small hyper-renegade molecule, gaseous form," I read out loud.

"But there were no traces of radioactivity," Gabi said.

"It was gas. Probably it rose. It must have been infinitesimal and extremely accelerated," I said, and started for the door.

"It's appearance was inevitable. It had to come up some place and time. Who knows from where it traveled, or from what time it came? We can only deal with the hyper-cancer that it caused. These people won't live more than five days. Order two units to stay and assist in cleanup and the disposal of the bodies and double check on radioactivity," I ordered Gabi.

Two familiar men stood near our EV and next to a fire where people waited to hear about the condition of their relatives. I had not seen them earlier, but I was sure that they would at least appear. Papá Damián and Grandfather Gregory waved. I got close enough to see Grandfather Gregory write down a few notes. I also knew that they felt deeply for these people. Perhaps they felt sorrow, an emotion that I had been reading about lately in grandfather Gregory's old paper books. As Gabi maneuvered our EV out of the

LLE, I watched the fires rise into the meteor-streaked night.

3

The day after the Chula Vista incident, I computerized my report and noted nothing uncommon about the sudden plague. I sent my observations simultaneously to the Los Angeles and Mexico City Research Centers. Often, I looked up at the thousands of volumes housed in Grandfather Gregory's library, paper books which were popular about fifty years ago, before computerized pocket books began to dominate the literary and spoken markets. I was surrounded by obsolete artifacts, which nevertheless gave joy to me, as I read them in the old fashioned way of reading. I concentrated on history and fiction and discovered very little difference in this oppositional binary that resisted separation. Perhaps I poorly invested countless hours enjoying the process of reading, of feeling the paper pages, of swallowing the words with my eyes and passing them to my brain. It was a wonderful sensation to read a book reproduced on real paper, rather than on a synthetic celluloid. It was a greater thrill and challenge to read the literary creations of my grandfather, a writer of novels who posited his vision of the future world.

He was simplistic, but strangely accurate. He recognized prospective political and economic changes and captured the nuances of the time and place in which he lived. His self-description, once computerized, was so intense that in hours he became a computer ghost and now appeared to assist and guide me through this world which I believed to be real. He emerged at the scenes which have occurred to me, many of which took place in the future of his books.

Grandfather Gregory and Papá Damián continuously pursued a better past. They understood that we created the past and not

141

the future in the present. Now, I too, strove for a better past. Into the computer in which he created his fiction and introduced his self-description, I computerized my reports. My history and my fiction simultaneously dwelt with him, not knowing for sure who had control of the vast knowledge banks at our command. People of Higher Existence possessed supercomputers and had access to the mega knowledge banks. Paper books were housed in one of nine archival museums of the Triple Alliance and recorded into mega-computers. Those who qualified and could afford it, paid for continuous updating. But I enjoyed reading Grandfather Gregory's paper books. I placed the cool, almost living skin-like paper to my lips and desired the people who resided in Grandfather Gregory's novel.

Gabi had stayed with me the evening of our return from Chula Vista. She was spending more time with me, watching over me, attempting to give me advice. "Are you reading those old books again?" Gabi asked disgusted.

I answered and watched her wrap a white bathrobe round her body. "It's a fetish I enjoy without shame."

"Soon you won't need them," Gabi said and reached for her computerized arm which was coupled to a portable electric update cube which she carried in our emergency vehicle. She rolled up the dangling right sleeve and reconnected the knowledge bank to her elbow. She quickly looked up and caught my indeterminate amazement as she finished the linking.

"Whether you like it or not," Gabi held her right arm up, "you don't have a choice."

"I have about a year to decide."

"If you refuse, I'll have your job. You'll be demoted to an emergency response crew, or worse, I'll fire you myself because my assistant must have a computerized arm."

Gabi moved closer. While she stared down at me, a wall of my grandfather's books framed her body. I returned to my reading. She went to the bedroom.

4

... Was I so consumed by the idea of professional success that I would sever my left arm to guarantee my position as medical director of the Los Angeles Mexico City Health Corridor? I answered "yes" to the third process Marine guard at the East Gate of the Camp Pendelton Marine Base and handed him our documentation, which initiated a meticulous five-minute security check. In a matter of seconds, they x-rayed us and our EV, and confirmed identification with our teeth and hair. At the end of five minutes, the final guard waved us through. As Gabi checked her right arm, making sure all systems functioned, I answered no to my original thought. I would not allow myself to be carved up and shaped into what the Directorate considered a model optimum efficient doctor. Voices from the past and present warned me not to allow them to deconstruct my humanity. I touched Gabi's left arm and slid my hand down to her fingers. She did not pull away. I stopped the vehicle. I let go of Gabi's hand and perceived her sadness.

The Legion of the Triple Alliance Soldiers arrived from the Philippine Islands, one of those countries whose territories we rented for military use and synchronously converted into a waste dump. We regularly supervised the ongoing physical and psychological examinations of incoming soldiers from the Pacific Basin areas, particularly the LLE zones. In this division there were quite a few unidentified strains of venereal infection and mental illness, certainly not uncommon.

Gabi and I walked through the incoming section of the hospital, where hundreds of soldiers angrily waited, resenting the physical processing they had to tolerate. I noticed their brown faces, similar to mine. These soldiers were "*mi raza*," as Grandfather Gregory had written. My race, I whispered. I stopped to listen to their conversation. They each spoke in Spanish about their wives, husbands, children, homes.

Most of this division originated from the Middle Life Existence Concentrations surrounding Mexico City. These troopers were but a few of the 20,000 who constituted one of the five hundred legions of the Triple Alliance Forces. Mexicans accounted for the ninety percent of the Triple Alliance armies. The other ten percent was made up of Canadian, USA and Mexican officers and administrative personnel. While I reviewed preliminary reports, I proceeded to eavesdrop; I understood that these soldiers did not complain about their duty, nor were they dissatisfied with their life condition. They missed their homes, their loved ones. They possessed the basic necessities of life that about thirty years past most Mexicans lacked. In the Americas and particularly in the countries of the Triple Alliance, hunger had been conquered and these soldiers were proof. Mexico's population was three times the size of the United States and Canada together, but almost all Mexicans lived a Middle Life Existence. They had access to the commodities and luxuries we enjoyed. The economic policies of the Triple Alliance had guaranteed a Middle Life Existence to people living within its borders. In Canada and the United States, individuals refused to volunteer, to serve in any way in the armed forces. After the establishment of the Triple Alliance and the access to military services, millions of Mexicans joined. To enhance their Middle Life Existence, they sent their salaries home. My country had prepared them for this role. Mexicans were highly trained and disciplined in militarized labors. Mutual respect endured between the Mexicans, Canadians and United Statesians, but there still persisted an attitude of apprehension, particularly toward the Mexicans. Gabi grabbed the report folder and handed me a slide.

"Check the white count," Gabi said.

"This guy is dead," I said, amazed.

"No, he's sitting right over here," Gabi said and led me to one of the youngest soldiers.

"He says he's feeling fine. Everything checks out. He wants to go home," Gabi reported.

"*¿De dónde eres joven?*" I asked, staring into his obsidian Asiatic eyes.

"*De la capital, doctor.*" Puzzled, he turned to his friends.

"Well, what's wrong with the kid's blood?" Gabi asked.

"You're the hematologist," I rebutted.

Before Gabi had a chance to respond, one of the staff doctors handed me the results of blood samples from about half of the legion. The three of us read them in utter shock. The majority of the soldiers had a severe leukemic blood count, but did not suffer any of the symptoms.

Gabi shook her head.

"I will not delay a whole legion," I said, realizing that I stood before a whole dormitory of nervous warriors.

"Select a rep sample and release the rest," I instructed the staff doctor. He left immediately.

On her computer arm, Gabi read the reports from the Los Angeles and Mexico City research centers. The Los Angeles returns were negative. The Mexico City findings indicated that the condition had surfaced recently, but neither the cause nor the cure was known, and the health of those who suffered the leukemic symptoms did not deteriorate. Gabi went to the EV and prepared to return to Temecula.

I walked over to a window and delighted in the sun high above the Pacific Ocean. Several large naval ships moved out to sea. A large flock of seagulls gracefully glided in to perch on the jagged bluff. I leaned my face toward the window and pressed my hands against the glass to feel the soothing warmth. To my left I saw the face of the young Mexican soldier.

"*Doctor, quiero volver a casa,*" the young soldier pleaded.

"*No se preocupe. Mañana volverá.* Tomorrow you'll be home,"

I answered.

The young soldier smiled and together we celebrated the sun.

5

Luckily, we received no emergency calls upon our return to Temecula. After I prepared dinner, I watered my potted roses, lay in bed with Gabi naked by my side and read one of grandfather's novels, entitled *A Rainbow of Colors*. It was about a French boy who was taken to live in Japan and became a master artist of the Japanese wood block print. He fell in love with a series of young Japanese males. The story was narrated by an American art collector, who was both attracted and repulsed by the life of the French artist. I read aloud the first few pages which contained a delightfully graphic description of an orgy in which grandfather's French artist found himself, to his delight, on his knees, wide eyed and opened mouth, staring at five engorged shiny penises. He joyfully sucked on each and everyone as they moved around him. All the while his American art collector friend observed scornfully.

"He must have sucked like this . . . "

Suddenly my erection was swallowed by Gabi's strong mouth and my grandfather's account of love and art in Japan was pushed aside by Gabi's vagina. I had no choice but to eat from her passionate gardens of charm.

Five-thirty in the morning, I awoke to Gabi's electrical arm pulsating the flashes of green light that indicated an urgent message. I shoved the hideous arm away. Throughout the night, repeatedly we had flared one another's flesh and quelled the fire with systematic multiple modes of copulations. She raised her arm to read the electronic missive which ordered us to report to the Los Angeles laboratories of the LAMEX Health Corridor. No explanation accompanied this order. It stood alone and we had to comply or suffer the corresponding demotion.

From the moment I felt the first warmth of the rising sun, the face of the pleasant smiling Mexican soldier pursued me. I didn't understand the importance of that chance meeting with that Mexican warrior. I sensed that a great and wonderful voyage had begun to unfold its path before me. Since our report time was three in the afternoon, Gabi decided to drive the surface streets to Los Angeles. We traveled through designated Middle Life Existence areas named for their old city names, Riverside, San Bernardino, East Los Angeles. As we neared Los Angeles and its massive ecumodern skyscrapers, we stopped for coffee. Monterey Park/East Los Angeles was a center for Mexican/Asian culture. Chinese, Japanese, Koreans and Southeast Asians had migrated in great numbers at the turn of the century. The Chinese had become the dominant force in sheer numbers.

After 1996, as I understood the novels of history, hundreds of thousands of mainland Chinese went to Taiwan, an island which became a transition center to the United States. In a few decades, millions of Chinese arrived in California. At one time there existed boat colonies consisting of hundreds of thousands of immigrants waiting to enter the United States. As the Chinese arrived, they settled next to Middle Life Existence areas made up of earlier Asian immigrants and long-time Mexican immigrants. By the year 2020, the Mexican population in the Los Angeles area grew to twenty-five million inhabitants. In order to survive and coexist, the Mexicans and Asians united economically, politically, culturally and racially. The common cross-cultural, racial marriages were between Asians and Mexicans.

Ted Chen was a third generation Chinese and Amalia, a native Mexican Californian. He and Amalia had been married for a little over a year and owned the house they used as a restaurant where Gabi and I entered for coffee that late morning. Antique oak tables and chairs, colorful leaded glass lamps, embroidered white tablecloths and delicate curtains made for a relaxing and comfortable place to eat and rest.

For me, their conversation served as a measure of the time, and revealed what most people were concerned about. People from the Middle Life Existence worried about the ecology of the Earth. They felt a real fear, an urgency to save what was left.

"Do you think we should bear children?" Amalia asked. We avoided the question by ordering a second cup of coffee. History had not changed the patterns for reproduction in our country. Lower Life Existence people had many children, Middle Life Existence folks bore barely enough to replace themselves and Higher Life Existence residents had practically none. Those people who decided on a family usually guaranteed that the child would receive the best of everything. A child was a long term investment, one they hoped would pay off. The Lower Life Existence dwellers conceived for the pleasure of having children. Their strength was in numbers.

Ted and Amalia accompanied us to the EV. As we left I viewed their image in the mirror. They were like the happy couples Grandfather described in his novels. Grandfather's characters married and had children without having to consider the ecology of the world. They simply neglected to pay much attention to it. I compared their world to ours and felt a tenderness for Ted and Amalia, who could not decide on a family. In Grandfather's days, marriage suggested forming a family. Today marriage meant sharing oneself with another.

"I hear the Navy can't contain a large waste strip which moves closer to shore every day," Ted said.

"A piece broke off and struck near San Diego. I hope they can stop it." Those were the last words I heard from Amalia as she waved goodbye.

The Chula Vista plague was what they referred to. Lately there had been a great deal of naval activity out at sea. But standard procedure was to warn us of impending danger. Gabi pursued the rumor through her information banks, but came up with a clear response. Ted and Amalia's statement stayed with me while we tested out through the elaborate security of the large laboratories of the LAMEX Los Angeles Research Center. I noticed that the employees worked at an ardent pace. On seeing this, we knew that whatever the occurrence, it was critical. Which explained why I had not been informed but instead *asked* to report to the center. In my office waited Gunther Ranph one of the Triple Alliance's best cranial commandos.

"What took you so long? We've been hit by the living shit," Gunther said softly.

I thought of Ted and Amalia and their hypothetical child. "Where did it strike?"

"Last reports are it hit just south of Ensenada and holding within a ten-mile circumference from point of contact with the shore. It's lethal. Not many survivors in the area." Gunther, the neurosurgeon, stood helpless.

"Has the area been secured?"

"The Directorate has sent Naval, Army and Medical security to surround the area. Nobody enters, nobody exits. It's horrible!" Gunther turned to Gabi. "It finally has happened. Our waste has turned against us," Gunther said as if confirming a prophecy.

The research center had automatically entered into a critical emergency state of operation. I left orders to be monitored every half hour on my way to the disaster site. As we made our way to the EV, Gunther approached carrying several medical bags.

"I want to go see for myself. You might need my help," Gunther said.

I gave Gunther permission to take his assistant and a fully equipped emergency vehicle. On our way to engage the supersonic travelway south, I noticed an uneasy stirring among the people in the streets. It was obvious that they felt some kind of disharmony. Through the glass of the EV, the eyes of insecurity and suspicion stared and passed into my thoughts. Happiness, a concept in Grand-father's fictions, seemed to be absent in their lives. People sought comfort and safety, not love or happiness. They aspired to a shelter from the individual and the collective disasters of life.

Beyond San Diego the sunlight collectors covering the Mexican hills shone in the late afternoon. We sped right through the Tijuana transition and the Pacific Rim Multinational manufacturing center. All along what used to be the border between the United States and Mexico, the *maquiladora* concept flourished. About twenty years after the turn of the century, the border became stabilized and eventually abolished. Although the border area had a few Lower Life Existence concentrations like Chula Vista, now all people lived a Middle Life Existence. Everyone worked in the manufacturing industry and seemed to be content. Poverty, hunger, crime had been eliminated by jobs. I recalled Grandfather's descriptions of how the Border Patrol tried to stop Mexican immigration into the United States and how the Immigration and Naturalization Service swept through Mexican neighborhoods arresting brown faced "illegal aliens." I laughed outloud at what time and history did. What irony that today the Mexican population dominated north of what once was the international border and that Euroamericans fled to the Mexican States of North Baja California and South Baja California. The Mexican debt of the twentieth century had been converted into beautiful Euroamerican Higher Life Existence concentrations. United States and Mexican contractors training and employing Mexican labor built family homes, condominiums and large ecumodern buildings that were in themselves small cities. Living on the relatively untouched Mexican coast was expensive and highly coveted.

We checked through the line of military personal surrounding Los Cinco Cielos, the Higher Life Existence area which had suffered the worst damage and casualties. Los Cinco Cielos, five ecumodern housing units capable of holding ten thousand families each, were self sufficient in every aspect of basic life necessities. The reports Gabi and I monitored indicated that Los Cinco Cielos housed some of the richest people of the LAMEX corridor.

We put on protective suits and masks, then stepped out into the contamination. Medical and military personal had evacuated survivors to a makeshift hospital just outside the ecumodern complex. I noticed the dead quickly being dissolved in chemical tankers brought in by the medical units. Thousands of decomposing bodies were huddled in groups in the center plaza of the five buildings. Although I was accustomed to death, this was far beyond my experience. Gabi's computerized arm flashed wildly as it received a rush of information. Gunther stood nearby, overpowered by the helplessness of the scene.

"What can we do?" Gabi asked.

Gunther farcically scratched his head, perhaps bewildered by Gabi's question. For a time, I don't know how long, we walked among the dead and the dying. We went through several of the outside family dwellings and discovered whole families who had died instantly from the initial wave of the effluvium. They perished in their activity, just as the people of Pompeii had. The three of us kept moving, realizing that, all the while, we had been giving orders to the dazed medical staff.

"The survivors require our help!" My scream seemed to jolt us out of the self-induced hypnotic state we were trained to impose on ourselves during situations of horror. We woke in the middle of the hospital and immediately went to work. As I contemplated the blackened feet of my first patient, a young woman of about twenty years, I heard a great crash. The military had just demolished one of the ecumodern habitats. In a few days, the area would be scraped clean. We humans had a bad habit of erasing the calamities caused by our mistakes; never did we learn from them. Gabi opened the right leg of a man who suffered from severe burns. She looked at me and I sensed she prepared to amputate. She retracted the scalpel and extracted a syringe from her computerized hand. She worked expertly and fast.

Near her Papá Damián and Grandfather Gregory were watching.
. . . Come and assist me, I thought, but instead they frantically wrote down everything they observed. Now I could use a computerized arm and hand, I thought. I felt a tug at my sleeve.

It was my patient who had chosen just then to lose the will to live.

7

Bulldozers worked through the night. By the next morning, three of the ecumodern buildings were pulverized. Salvageable steel and other metals were separated and airlifted out by cargo helicopters that blew the smoke and ashes of the cremated into the air and out to the polluted sea. By the third day, the putrid gases seemed to have dissipated and the black living sludge to have dried, splintered, penetrated the Earth and vanished. Beyond the shore, the surface of the ocean gleamed. On the fifth day, Gabi, Gunther and I had treated about eighty percent of the injured. There were more survivors than first estimated. The last five hundred were severe head injuries. They were cases on which I had to decide whether to end their suffering or allow Gunther to attempt a reorganization of their brain.

I reviewed each case with Gunther and Gabi and finally concluded that about twenty-five had a chance to regain a normal neurological life. It simply came down to a choice. Those people who were injured too seriously, we treated last in hopes that they would die. But unlike my first patient, their will to live was strong. Consequently, I injected four hundred, and within minutes Mexican soldiers took their bodies to the crematorium. Euthanasia was part of my medical training. I'm sure that these people agreed with my decision. The injuries they suffered had rendered them idiots, living vegetables. I had made a scientific decision that I was trained to make and live with.

Of the twenty-five, we began with the patient we thought had the best chance for survival. Gabi and I assisted Gunther as he pressed down with his scalpel on the patient's scalp, the thickest skin on the human body, until it parted to expose the pale pink bone of the skull. Gabi had prepared the brace and bit. Gunther leaned on the skull bone, drilled four holes and with a saw connected the perforations and retracted the skull plate, thus exposing the brain.

"Get ready for some big action," Gunther said joyfully.

For fifteen hours straight, Gabi and I worked with Gunther. He seemed to gain more energy from each skull he sawed open. His biggest test came with a ten-year-old girl who had already survived one aneurysm, which was caused by vapors she had inhaled. He opened the skull and penetrated through the brain's natural divisions, searching for the stem of the bleeding. I noticed the remarkable pliability of the brain as Gunther moved the brain structures. Suddenly, with a slight move of an instrument, the hemorrhaging became a torrent of blood.

"What a gusher!" Gunther stepped back, took a deep breath and without any hesitation asked Gabi for a clip and guided it down the heavy stream of blood, letting the clip squeeze shut. He pulled his red hands back and waited. The bleeding stopped. This particular child lived. In the days that followed, we lost seven of the weaker patients. I ordered Gunther, our beloved cranial commando, to accompany these patients to a San Diego health clinic and from there to return to Los Angeles.

Exactly seven days after the disaster, we discovered that most of the survivors had neurological damage and were suffering from progressive retardation, some faster than others. We left the area clean, except for about three hundred survivors who had escaped before and during our presence. As we made preparations for departure, some approached and watched. The lethargic body movements and the slur in speech revealed the progressive brain damage. In saving lives, we had created a colony of what the Directorate identified as "primitives." What became of that colony I don't particularly want to know.

I was curious about the ten-year-old girl that Gunther saved. One thing I remembered was that the blood she received during the operation came from a new batch. The blood was given by Mexican soldiers from Mexico City. I checked the blood count and it was exactly the same as the smiling Mexican soldier's I met at Camp Pendleton Marine base. The last report I read had indicated that the girl had recovered one hundred percent.

8

Two weeks passed and the central office in Los Angeles was quiet. No emergency had been reported. No disaster to interrupt my physical and mental rest. I was glad to have time for myself, time before I would go to my Mexico City office. Other than the regular daily computer reports, nothing extraordinary was communicated. The two week pause permitted Gabi to visit a friend in Los Angeles.

During this time, I read from Grandfather's work, I worked in the garden surrounding the house and often took walks along the border of the Oakridge Ranch Estates. Still, the blood count of the Mexican soldier persisted in my thoughts. One morning by the back side of the ranch I climbed a steep hill and discovered to my amazement a horse's skeleton. Some of the bones seemed to be pulverized and still others crumbled into dust when I disturbed their rest. I returned to the house and called the Ranch patrol to tell them of my gruesome discovery. The voice on the line said that they would dispose of the remains immediately.

I spent my days reading the old books and studying in my Grandfather's library. I read the history of his time, about how the post-industrial revolution struck in the twilight of the twentieth century and about the radical changes that occurred in society.

In one of Grandfather's manuscripts, a 400-page novel entitled *The Rag Doll Plagues*, he described a humid, tropical, drizzly afternoon in Orange County, where in the cancer unit of a large university hospital, experimental treatments were given to about five hundred terminally ill patients and five hundred newly identified cancer victims. On the morning of that tropical day, the one thousand sufferers were given an experimental drug developed from antibiotic poison

plants, hybridized at the university. These one thousand patients
had signed a release and agreement that they would take whatever
drug or treatment the cancer specialist prescribed. When offered
this new synthetic chemical, they were not told what they ingested.
They only were informed that all one thousand patients in the section
were given the same experimental drug and dosage. By one o'clock
in the afternoon, half of the worst of the terminally ill began to ask
for water. That morning most of them were so weak they could
hardly speak and by three they sat up in bed, asked for lunch and
talked about the future with the astonished nurses and doctors. By
early evening, all five hundred terminals were threatening to leave
the hospital. By six, university police were called in to maintain
calm and prevent the patients from leaving. However, before the
police had arrived about one hundred and fifty patients left, wearing
whatever garments they found. By now the whole cancer unit had
heard about the cure and insisted on their clothes to leave. The
transformation of the dying patients was so radical that the whole
medical staff and the patients were talking about the miraculous
cancer cure. Finally after years of research, they had conquered
the deforming plague of cancer. The fatal grimaces had been transformed to happy faces. At seven in the evening, the one thousand
cancer survivors began to walk out of the hospital. Many were restrained by the police, but many others escaped. The news had
spread throughout the hospital that a cure had been found. Every
severely ill patient, regardless of whether he suffered from terminal
cancer or not, wanted the cure. At nine o'clock, the city police and
county sheriffs arrived to face a full-fledged riot.

The people who escaped the experiment had gone home to
their families, informing anyone who listened about the miraculous
drug. The television news stations reacted promptly. Interviews
with the patients preempted regular programming. In a matter of
hours, cancer patients throughout the United States swarmed to the
nearest hospital, demanding that they be given the experimental
chemical. When it was a question of life, the people displayed no

fear of the enforcement institutions and they began to take over hospital quarters, drug stores, doctor's offices and clinics. Some doctors were even kidnapped and held for ransom for the cancer-curing drug. Several doctors were murdered because officials had not responded to their captor's demands. In numerous cases, both patients and hostages died because the cure had not been made available in time to save a life. The tragedies multiplied as the days passed. In two weeks it was reported that the original takers of the medication had begun to die suddenly.

The citizenry aggressively accused the government and the multinational drug producers of withholding chemicals in certain parts of the world in order to maintain profit margins and in other areas of the globe to control population. As a whole, the population was convinced that cancer had been cured, but political and economic factors out of their control resulted in the medications not being released to save lives. People in the United States lived longer, there were great organizations of Old People Power.

No matter the cost, everybody wanted to be young and live forever. Soon the newspaper and television photos of the dead original patients were everywhere and the demand for the miraculous cancer cure subsided. Further clandestine experimentation on the chemical and the patients continued, but the results never were reported nor published. Shortly thereafter, the populace forgot about the cancer cure. Nonetheless, the year-round government-sponsored, 24-hour cancer telethon continued.

As I read *The Rag Doll Plagues*, I grasped my inability to discern fact from fiction. Grandfather Gregory's novel became a history. I began to read exclusively for the pleasure of information and not for the pleasure of entertainment nor for psychological avoidance. Midway through the novel I came across a description of an AIDS camp established in 1999 at Asilomar, California.

There the University of California conducted experimentation on the disease and on the process of dying. In 1995, a riot broke out in the homosexual community of San Francisco. The citizenry went into the Moribundus Support Houses, which were financed by public funds to assist AIDS patients suffering the last stages of the disease. AIDS, like cancer, was a deforming, hideous infection which slowly transformed the individual into a social pariah. At that time San Francisco housed the largest concentration of AIDS patients in the country. Without warning, the outside community attacked and brutally dragged out to the street every AIDS victim in the Moribundus Support Houses and systematically massacred them.

Shortly after the mass murders, the state and local authorities intervened and ordered all reported HIV-infected persons to be rounded up and sent to the Asilomar resort for their own protection. The other states followed suit and arranged to help finance a national AIDS settlement at Asilomar. In one year, almost all the AIDS patients were housed at Asilomar. Those who went underground were given one month to surrender or face the death penalty. The logic behind this concentration camp alternative was that it was the only way to control the AIDS plague.

The beautiful shoreline property of Asilomar belonged to the University of California, which donated it for the right to conduct experiments on AIDS. At the turn of the century the university scientists announced that AIDS was caused by a polluted mutant gene that originally appeared in Pittsburgh, had been taken to Africa where it germinated into a stronger lethal virus, and finally had been returned to the United States. Upon reading about the inhumane treatment of AIDS victims, I could not believe that this could have happened in the United States.

As I read Grandfather's descriptions and testimony of the surviving AIDS patients, who were allowed to leave Asilomar to die privately in their homes, I tried to convince myself that I was reading fiction. Nonetheless, according to Grandfather, these were actual interviews preserved in the University of California library. By the year 2003, Asilomar cremated its last experimental AIDS patient. HIV-positive people were considered polluting factors and extremely dangerous.

I left Grandfather's library on Sunday morning and calculated that I had spent several days reading the old books in the old way. I reassured myself that cancer and AIDS had been cured and that the drugs to cure these diseases were available at any pharmacy, day or night, for anyone to purchase.

I found myself outside enjoying the morning chill and the rising sun. The EV was parked in the garage. Gabi had returned. To the smell of burning flesh I rushed into the house and found Gabi recharging her computer arm. Her face showed fatigue. She appeared older. I didn't know her age and it didn't matter. To me Gabi was immortal. I smiled as I wondered what delightful sins she had enjoyed with her friends. For a few more days, Gabi and I enjoyed the pleasures of an ecological life.

9

Even with a population of one hundred million, life in Mexico City was unpredictable and exhilarating. The city had developed into a Pacific Basin cultural hub, where the talented people of the world congregated. Artists and artisans came to show off their flair. The Triple Alliance had several large art museums dedicated to its own artists. In the past two decades, the symbol makers theorized, intellectualized and directed art to primarily the Middle Life Existence folks. As I walked by the massive Paz Museum of Modern Art, I observed the Mexicans rushing to their homes, jobs or recreation centers. Although Mexico City was a Middle Life Existence concentration, it had the sensation of a Lower Life Existence area, a prison camp with the energies of rebellion seething just below the surface. I experienced this sensation regularly and I was convinced that this feeling came about because of the repressed history the city rested upon. Ancient times and cultures issued forth from deep within the soul of the Mexican earth. It was a past ignored, but felt deeply, an ancient fervor that ran through the mind, heart and blood of Mexico. Since the time of Tenochtitlan to today's Mexico City, the Mexicans continually carried their historical ghosts dangling from their modern ritualistic necklaces.

The city, situated at 7,200 feet above sea level, lay in the middle of a seismic bowl surrounded by mountains and majestic volcanoes. To the Mexican people it represented the center of the world and to the Triple Alliance and the Pacific Basin countries it functioned like the Los Angeles to San Diego area, as a political, economic and cultural core. For over one hundred years people migrated to the city in search of jobs.

For a time, it was the fastest developing city in the world. It overdeveloped into chaos and the lowest quality of urban life in the Triple Alliance. As the population grew, the ecological balance of the city was destroyed, its public services overwhelmed and natural resources decimated. Above all, water had been the greatest problem facing humanity, which covered the planet's surface. By 2050, two massive breeder reactors were constructed on the Pacific Coast. The largest, El Mejiquito generated electricity and purified and pumped water directly to Mexico City. Ironically, I read in grandfather Gregory's books that the city was built on a lake and continued to sink for hundreds of years. Mexicans had lived contented in this quagmire for the last one hundred years. Up to now, no mass riots, protests or threats had vexed the Mexican central government. Mexicans, like United Statesians and Canadians had lived in a perpetual hypnosis for more than a century. I don't know when humanity gave up exactly, but we had lost the ability and desire to complain.

Mexico City was the most contaminated city of the Triple Alliance.

Yesterday, at nine in the morning, on my walk to the LAMEX research center, I glanced at the sun as it appeared like a moon through the worst polluted air in the Americas. Daily, a brownish haze covered the Valley of Mexico. This thick smog consisted of thousands of tons of metals, chemicals, bacteria and dirt so thick that it darkened the sky like mahogany. Nonetheless, the Mexicans had lived in this irreversibly polluted toxic air for more than a century. These conditions were responsible for the steady rise of human biological mutations.

Although the streets and plazas were relatively clean, the air and water were irreversibly contaminated. Worst of all was the horrid smell of dried excrement and bacteria that the northeast winds brought to cover the valley with an inch or more of virulent dust. In Mexico City everything oscillated: the earth, the layers of dust, the waves of heavy air, the plagues of flies and rats, the massive buildings, the concrete sidewalks and the dead trees.

The city, completely bare of vegetation, caused the herbivorous animals to become carnivorous. Weak animals were devoured by the stronger. Frail humans were either confined for the rest of their life to an indoor existence or risked the danger of lethal infection outside. Mexico City was the only Middle Life Existence city where "quality of life" referred exclusively to economic indoor living. Only people who had to be outside ventured into the streets for long periods of time. Yet millions of people worked, played, loved and died here.

Although it was garbage pickup day, I was unruffled by the odor and immensity of the horrible human refuse, and enjoyed the walk to my office at the research center. Twice a week large trucks drove tons of waste out to the garbage colonies, where millions of people scavenged and lived off the salvageable waste.

My administrative stay in the city was scheduled for one week, but because of the blood research that I conducted and my interest in the new clinics in the colony of El Pepenador situated in the area of the garbage people, I prolonged my stay. I suggested to Gabi that we visit the clinic. Earlier in the week they had reported a rash of three hundred fatalities of children, each less than a year old. Life conditions in this area were repulsive. Yet the people seemed to be very healthy. El Pepenador was infamous for the unpredictable biochemical fires that often lasted for weeks. Gabi's research revealed that most of the weak children of the garbage zones died soon after birth, but if they lived beyond nine months to a year in the severely polluted environment of El Pepenador, survival was ninety percent certain.

We discovered that the three hundred children had died from an infection that liquified the lungs; literally the children had drowned. When Gabi and I arrived, five children were still alive, three near death. I went to the two stronger children, a boy and a girl. Gabi estimated that the other three would die before dawn. Without Gabi's knowing, I ordered blood counts on three adults in the colony.

Three adult men volunteered. I was not surprised to discover that the blood condition of these men was exactly like the severe anemic state of the Mexican soldier in San Diego. Impossible to explain, but they seemed perfectly healthy and did not suffer any adverse symptoms from their condition. I ordered immediate transfusions from the healthy adult men to the two sick children. Shortly after one in the morning, we finished. By five in the morning the three critically ill children expired. But the transfused boy and girl steadily improved. The next day the boy died suddenly and the girl got out of bed and asked to go home.

The boy should have lived, I thought. I gave Gabi permission to return to the Mexico City research center to correct a malfunction in her arm. I decided to stay and ordered one mobile lab to remain.

In the days following Gabi's departure, I felt myself free to carry out experiments on one thousand blood samples from the people of El Pepenador. I tested for foreign chemicals and metals in the blood and discovered that other than the normal contaminants, there was a high concentration of lead in the blood, which seemed to have no ill effects, neither physically nor mentally. With every sample I studied, my excitement increased at what I found. Something wonderful, biologically wonderful, had occurred to some of the people of Mexico City. Some time in the recent past, a great chemical transformation had taken place.

Upon testing the last sample, I was convinced that I had stumbled upon a biochemical quantum jump. These people with whom I had lived for the past five days had been transformed genetically to produce a blood that was able to sustain life in the most polluted conditions on earth. I did not know what agent or combination of chemicals or processes caused this miraculous condition. But at this point, I was sure that deep in the molecules of the blood of these people, there existed an agent or agents that cured some severe lung diseases.

Gabi had maintained communication and I suggested that she continue her work at the research center while I carried on my evaluation of the health conditions at El Pepenador. In our last communication she asked about the girl's status and, upon answering, I realized that I had commited a terrible mistake. I had let the child go and I had failed to test the dead boy's blood. With great fear, I asked if the boy's cadaver had been cremated.

I was lucky, the boy's remains had been held for seven days for identification and claim, and no one had come forth. As for the girl, the medical team at the clinic ordered a location survey. Within an hour of my request, they had positioned her dwelling.

That evening I destabilized the boy's frozen cadaver. I tested the blood to find that the fibrenogen had run amuck and coagulated the blood almost instantaneously after achieving red cell incompatibility. But why had the girl survived?

I decided to go to her dwelling place immediately, but as I moved to my door, I stumbled and fell to the floor. I felt weak and feverish and realized that I had hardly eaten in four days. I stayed on the floor and fell asleep.

By eight the next morning, I was arriving near the child's dwelling place. Upon my entering into the work areas of the dump, miles and miles of immense waste mounds, which had accumulated for more than one hundred years, rose like giant tortoises which undulated as I moved forward.

That morning the winds shifted, cleared the Anahuac Valley of the thick smog and revealed the blue of the sky and the brilliance of the sun. It had been months since the people of Mexico City had seen a clear sky. When the blue of the sky appeared, the workers took the day to spend with their families, to picnic and give thanks for life.

This spontaneous celebration reminded me of Grandfather's descriptions of the Thanksgiving ritual. It was a ritual long forgotten after the great catastrophe. Now humanity celebrated the erratic appearance of the sky and the sun. How pitiful! Perhaps it was only I who made these comparisons, for it was only I who accessed Grandfather's books. I compared his present to mine. I found

it strange, but not any better. I rested and wiped my brow. The
temperature rose to well over one hundred degrees and the waste
I walked on continually stirred. From the top of one of the higher
mounds I located a cluster of dwellings. I checked the computerized
map, which indicated that there ahead I would find the child.

Twenty-five dome-like dwellings made of cloth and metal made
up the cluster to which the child's family had been assigned. Five
people—a man, two women and two children—sat with legs crossed
at the entrance to the child's home. I immediately recognized the
girl.

"Good blue day," I said as I extended my open hands, palms
up to the sky.

The man looked at the girl and the women. A few words were
exchanged and the girl I sought went to sit next to him as he motioned
me forward to join them. I sat down, tired, on the white canvas
material woven from cloth and metal. Oddly cool to the touch,
it refreshed me. The women extended a drink, which I accepted
without any hesitation.

The man broke the silence. "You cured our child and we are
thankful."

My eyes ventured beyond him and watched a distant mound
of waste swell while children played on it. Nearby, adults ate and
conversed. Life here was tranquil and good. These people appeared
clean, healthy and content.

"What do you want with our daughter?" asked one of the women,
while she filled my glass again. Only a few drops of blood, I thought.
I felt ridiculous making the request.

"You want her blood!" Incredulous, the man raised his voice.
Yet there was no anger in his tone.

"Only a few drops."

The woman seemed relieved. "The child will give you a vial of
her blood. We owe her life to you, doctor."

I took the samples as soon as possible. The blood smears
confirmed what I suspected. The fibrenogen was normal and she

possessed an extremely high white corpuscle count. I could see the smiling Mexican soldier's face blend into the girl's countenance. Could this agent carry the notion of gender? That was the key, the agent had gender and the transfusions could not be made from male to male, nor female to female, but from male to female or female to male. Gender and sexuality allowed it to reproduce naturally.

My restless expression revealed the excitement I felt. I had discovered a radical change in the human immune system. It was so obvious but so well hidden by the centuries of prejudicial attitude toward the Mexicans.

But it was their blood that allowed them to survive in this hyperbolically contaminated city. I was convinced that their blood could save the lives of thousands dying from pulmonary diseases.

That night I found myself wrapped in a wonderfully baroque cover made from a multitude of colorful waste materials. I was not allowed to return until morning, for at night crossing the garbage areas was extremely dangerous. I listened to the family sleep and to the sounds of El Pepenador wasteland. I rested my eyes on the children and I marvelled at the immaculateness of the dwelling. My eyes became heavy and as I faded, Grandfather Gregory stopped writing and lay down beside me.

10

A computerized arm like Gabi's could have made it easier to test the blood of the Pepenador family. With that arm, everything was at my disposal. I could access whatever information possibly held in computers. Twice on this trip, a computer arm would have come in handy. I was finally back in Los Angeles and back to work at the Los Angeles Research Center. Our trip from Mexico City was uneventful. I had enjoyed myself wonderfully and went to several nocturnal Ritual Clubs where music, dance, sex, drugs, violence, etc., were merchandised for those who were entertained by reliving the thrills of the negative traditions of times long past.

I enjoyed the music and the dances, the sex only with Gabi. Although she enjoyed other people, I believed she cared for and wanted to be with me. I went to the Ritual Clubs to be with her. We all had our habits. Mine had become Gabi and reading Grandfather Gregory's paper books.

In a way, I was familiar with the Ritual Clubs for their offerings were similar to the sex, drugs and violent worlds which I found in the books in Grandfather's library. The few nights Gabi and I spent in Mexico City compared to the willing degradation of the characters in *Long Live Music*, a novel written more than a century ago by an obscure Columbian writer who committed suicide at the age of twenty-five. I remember that fast text, the attraction which the heroine had to extreme degeneracy and perversion. How sweet the music, the partying, the ritualizing, I thought, as I whirled the Pepenador blood round and round in a glass test tube.

Gabi and I spent three days at El Rancho de los Revueltas. We went for walks in the early evening and in the brief coolness of the dawn we jogged four miles to Lake Skinner to watch the brilliant sunrise. She worked on her experiment notes and finished reports. To her annoyance, I continued to peruse the books in the library. No matter what we did, the Pepenador blood back at the L.A. lab never deserted my thoughts. I searched desperately for a clue as to what I should do with the knowledge that I safeguarded. What I had discovered terrified me. In the written text, there exists an answer, I thought. Before me there appeared Papá Damián and Grandfather Gregory. They floated over to a series of shelves that I had never explored. The books were dusty and streaked with strong cob webs.

"In macabre creations you will find a plan," Papá Damián spoke as Grandfather Gregory pointed to a book hidden in the deepest part of the shelf. I reached in for the book and a large black spider guarding its clothy white cocoons clung to my right hand. Startled, I pulled my hand back. I felt the sting and shook the arachnid to the floor. Damn you, I thought, and violently crushed the hard poisonous insect. Immune to all common insect poisons, I was most annoyed at being caught by surprise. My anger subsided.

I dusted off the book and read its title: *Frankenstein Or The Modern Prometheus.*

And so it was that a Gothic romance which first appeared in 1818 and described the creation of an artificial man, a new man, constructed from parts of corpses, posited the information that I sought. I, like Doctor Frankenstein, decided to conduct clandestine experiments, but unlike the good doctor, I needed living people to give blood and terminally ill patients for experimental subjects. As I put the novel down I knew that the monster I could create was not an individual man, but a reaction to the knowledge I possessed.

Across the library, the delicate fragrance of burning flesh proclaimed the presence of Gabi with her constructed body dressed to venture back to the Ritual Clubs of Los Angeles. The greater my obsession, the more I desired her, but intellectually I was not yet willing to reveal my secret. The strong presence of Papá Damián and Grandfather Gregory encouraged me to proceed with my work.

Grandfather Gregory continued to write while Gabi smiled, answering a call from her computerized arm. She went off pursuing the sunset down into the polluted Los Angeles basin.

"Return to your people," Grandfather Gregory whispered the last words I heard that night.

11

I appeared peculiarly disheveled to Ted and Amalia Chen, whom I had decided would be the people to share my discovery. They, more than anyone, would understand and help me with my plan of experimentation. I had arrived late in the evening to the couple's house, located between a Middle Life and a Lower Life Existence concentration, ideal for the experiments I wanted to conduct on human subjects.

They were at first surprised to hear of my desire to enter the *barrio* to identify patients with pulmonary ailments and blood donors.

"We don't want to cause the destruction of human life by experimentation," Amalia said.

"Your involvement might help save lives!"

Ted and Amalia escorted me to the guest room where, unable to sleep, I wrote down the procedures I was to follow the next day.

By the early morning hours I finally fell asleep only to be awakened by a loud discussion carried on by several people in Ted and Amalia's restaurant. What sounded to me like an argument had transformed into laughter and joviality from a man sipping tea and sitting cross-legged on the floor in the middle of the restaurant. The early morning customers breakfasted and conversed with a dark white haired man who was introduced as Don Antonio Pérez, resident of the Lower Life Existence known as El Mar de Villas, a *barrio* which I had identified as a possible place to conduct my experiments.

Ted and Amalia explained to Don Antonio my purpose and he volunteered to guide us to El Mar de Villas infirmary where a man, a dear friend of his, lay on his deathbed.

172

Don Antonio, himself a master *curandero*, had tried to cure his friend by using modern and ancient treatments available to him, but all efforts failed against the infection caused by the pernicious gas cloud that had attacked his friend. At first sight Don Antonio inspired confidence and trust. After coffee and sweet bread, the Chen's closed their house restaurant and the four of us entered the outskirts of El Mar de Villas.

The entrance to El Mar de Villas was a wide street that at one time functioned as a freeway. But after the ecological disasters and demographic change in the Los Angeles area, nobody wanted to get to where the freeway led. It was a road abandoned to gradual decay. Along the way, thousands of small crosses draped in artificial flowers and jammed into the soft earth alongside the concrete stood as memorials to the people who had died on their journeys. These *descansos* marked the resting places of the victims of diseases caused by the production of lethal debris.

Access to the center of El Mar de Villas was through a colorful passage of dancing *descansos* for the dead. Beyond them there was life, crowded into small quarters, existing happily. As we walked through the residence areas, I noticed the severe concentration of humanity in each unit, every bit of space compartmentalized and livable. Even more amazing was the universal profusion of color that decorated every object deep in El Mar de Villas and which made us walk slower as we penetrated to the heart of the Lower Life Existance Concentration.

"Your eyes will adjust to the chromatics," Don Antonio said as he acknowledged the people who bowed their heads as he passed. I had never visited such a remarkable space. The practicality of the objects was simple. What struck me were the brilliant windows made from the glass of broken bottles. Ted and Amalia, who had never traveled this far into the Lower Life Existence concentration, had been mute since we began our ingress. We found that talk was superfluous to express what we saw, felt and thought. We seemed to be communicating through sight and touch channeled through

Don Antonio. We were unaware that we traveled for several hours, but the three of us knew that our destination was near. By now I understood that Don Antonio was special to the residents of El Mar de Villas and that he commanded the physical presence of power. The visual, auditory, palpable, olfactory dimensions of power were his. I sensed that to address him was to engage in a ritual of the highest order for the people of El Mar de Villas.

Immediately upon his arrival to the center, his followers gathered around him and transformed his body by bestowing on him the finery of sacred dress, by placing next to him sacred relics and by performing festive liturgies which included a welcome for his guests. I understood that I was in the presence of the Man-god of El Mar de Villas and that I was about to meet what now had become his uncommon patient.

The crowd outside Don Antonio's residence grew as word circulated that a doctor had come to cure Don Antonio's child. Don Antonio escorted us to a room decorated with fresh flowers and fruits. At the center, there lay an immaculately white child of about 11 years old.

The extraordinarily beautiful young boy drank water as we entered his presence. The people of El Mar de Villas, where the boy was born and destined to become the next Man-god, wanted me to cure him. Perhaps it was Don Antonio who beckoned me to approach the child.

Fear had for an instant filled my ears.

Within two hours, I was certain the child suffered from severe emphysema. During my diagnosis, I thought of Gabi and her computer arm. With that arm I could have had the results of the analysis much faster. I was too slow. People were impatient. The results were conclusive, emphysema, caused by some unknown gaseous agent.

While I examined the child, Don Antonio's voice addressed my powers as healer; my charge was to cure the child at all cost. Ted and Amalia had become observers and waited for my orders. As I worked, Don Antonio's voice entered and exited my thoughts, but not until he asked a proper question did I respond to him.

"Yes, I need blood. Go to your people and get at least ten men and women born in Mexico City, and whose parents were born there as well. Try to find people who have just come from the capital. We need their blood if we are to save the child."

The response was immediate. Within hours, hundreds of people had volunteered to donate blood. By late that night, I had collected and tested enough to perform a complete transfusion. The blood from these people was exactly the same as that of the smiling soldier and the Pepenadores. At one in the morning, I called Ted and Amalia to assist me and asked Don Antonio to tell his people to retreat from their vigil. I asked for quiet and not to be disturbed. Don Antonio responded to my request and then posted himself at the door of the small room where I had begun the transfusion procedure.

With the completion of the procedure, daylight struck the heart of El Mar de Villas and it seemed that with the sun's illumination the child became stronger. By mid-morning, the child's breathing was nearing normal and Ted, Amalia and I had breakfast with Don Antonio. Outside, the people rejoiced and celebrated the salvation of their future Man-god. Don Antonio did not inquire whether I had used a drug to cure the child.

"Whatever the secret you possess, guard it well, for it can lead to great harm as well as good," Don Antonio said as he left us at the border of El Mar de Villas.

As Ted, Amalia and I walked away, I turned to capture the last of the brilliant colors of Don Antonio's Lower Life Existence concentration. I was amazed and thrilled by the indiscriminate splashing of the crimson.

At the house restaurant, Ted prepared a succulent meal of Mexican and Chinese cuisine. I had never tasted such exquisite flavors. I probably had not eaten for days. My body had adjusted to ingesting little food, but today I felt as if I could never be satisfied. The taste of those foods lingered in my mouth when I entered my office at the LAMEX research center. I smiled at the thought of that gluttonous meal, of my success with the ill child.

12

About three weeks after my encounter with the El Mar de Villas child, I was asked to examine a female black patient of twenty-two years who suffered from chronic chest congestion, accompanied by coughing and bleeding. For six months, she had suffered pain and severe loss of weight. Her parents were desperate and asked to speak with me. Our discussion was brief and my response was direct and candid. Their description and the medical records which I studied briefly indicated that their daughter had but a few days to live. Here again, I acquiesced to treat an irreversible case and I made the Nortons understand that my ability to save their daughter was nonexistent, to prolong her life less than one percent, to ease her pain and help her die inevitable. Under these conditions, I went to see Lyn Braze Norton at her parents home at the Higher Life Existence city of Newport Beach.

I ordered one EV and complete Mobile Lab to the Norton home and I located Gabi at Temecula. She was excited that I had called, and speaking with her heightened my spirits.

I directed her to meet me at the Nortons.

Gabi's voice sounded fatigued and depressed. Perhaps she was experiencing a withdrawal from the chemicals she ingested at the Los Angeles Ritual Clubs. I needed her scientific expertise and her physical company. I had decided then that I would share my secret with her. Gabi was waiting when I arrived. Without saying a word, we embraced and walked in together.

Immediately, we were overcome by the immensity of the beveled glass entry way, a lofty corridor into a different world. The Nortons, exquisitely dressed in evening apparel, guided us through a dwelling dominated and decorated with white objects in white-walled and glass rooms.

These people were the rich of the late twenty-first century. They looked forward to enhancing their holdings well into the twenty-second century.

Out of sinful curiosity, I had requested some background information on the Nortons and had discovered that Mr. Norton's family wealth had been made from the construction of the underground Middle Life Existence communities in the upper California deserts. He and his brothers held substantial interest in these areas and more subsurface dwellings had been approved by State legislation.

Mrs. Norton, a recent entrepreneur, had amassed a fortune by winning the Triple Alliance contracts to export medical wares during the recent Love War between Paraguay and Brazil. The Love Wars were a phenomena of the times. I for one preferred them to the terror of the twentieth century described in Grandfather Gregory's books.

The austere immaculate windows and white rooms pained my eyes. Not a word was said as we followed the Nortons, who moved briskly, assuredly, as if no one was dying in their house, to where their daughter sat.

Facing the sun above the sea, Lyn Braze Norton invited us to sit by her.

Several small boats circled an area over buildings that had been submerged by the relentless rising of the sea. Divers went down in hopes of finding abandoned jewels, something of value or mere interest, a chrono object of a drowned chronotope in our time.

The Nortons opened the sliding glass doors. The breeze was warm, accompanied by the delicate music of crystal chimes decorating one of the patio tables.

Gabi's voice responded to an introduction. She nudged me towards Lyn's ice-cold hand. Gabi's computerized arm began the preliminary exam. Lyn rested comfortably as I administered the blood transfusion one hour later.

"Gregory, she'll die if you transfuse this blood. I've checked it all. It's mostly white blood cells! And something else is wrong, but I can't find what it is! It's peculiar," Gabi whispered angrily. I smiled and took her outside to listen to the beautiful crystal chimes.

"Gabi, please. I have done this before. If I were to tell you what I think I have discovered, you would not believe me. Let me go on with this treatment. If she is not better within twelve hours you can turn me in to the authorities and take over."

"Gregory, I'll be considered negligent if you fail," Gabi said. She moved to the white marble railing. The sun fell slowly behind her.

"Your choice," I said and started for the door. Gabi remained behind.

All the while, the Nortons watched as I carried the transfusion of Mexican blood. The two Mobile Lab assistants came in to monitor the patient, while outside Gabi waited for Lyn's and my fate.

The wind picked at the chimes. They sang an uncontrolled symphony. The sea saturated the air. All of us tasted and smelled the ocean. The waves crashed onto the shore. A southern storm approached. I watched Gabi examine Lyn, who spoke of her feeling stronger to her astonished parents.

Twelve hours later, Lyn grew stronger. With their voices competing with the chimes, the Nortons viewed their daughter as if she were a newborn or traveling through her last moments of life. In her magnificent home on a bluff above what at one time was Pacific Coast Highway, Lyn watched back. The faces of her parents beamed at their surviving child. The two assistants waved that they would wait outside for further orders. Gabi turned away from the Nortons, smiled, shook her head in disbelief and came outside where the wind from the sea changed direction and became caressingly warmer, like Lyn Braze Norton, who seemed to talk her way out of death.

"You hyped the blood! You hyped the blood! She'll degenerate again. How could you do that!" Gabi said as she watched the

Nortons, who were oblivious to what happened outside.

"No, it's the blood that is helping Lyn," I said confidently.

"Don't be absurd! That's impossible!" Gabi tensed her lips.

"The blood that I used somehow fights off lung diseases. This blood has changed biologically. It's not the same as ours. Gabi, I believe I have found a human quantum biological leap, maybe a radical adaptation or even a mutation. Whatever we call it, this blood seems to cure lung diseases."

"Where in the hell did you get this blood?"

"Sure. I'll tell you."

Gabi began to listen while inside Lyn Braze Norton, for the first time in months, stood under her own strength. She smiled and, like that Mexican soldier, her face filled with the radiance of the exalted sun.

13

I was alone, more than ever before. I had discovered a biological change that occurs once in a millennium. This knowledge threw me into an abyss of loneliness, emptiness. The renegade blood of Mexicans who for almost two and a half centuries lived under the surmising eye of the United States, had now given the world an unbelievable gift. I was the first to understand the potential healing power that it offered.

What counted was the discovery, not who found the offering. For thousands of years, on authorities' terms, whether by a high Aztec priest or a United States or Mexican president, Mexicans have offered their blood to the world and to the sun only to be exploited and manipulated. Mexican blood paid the price: human sacrifice, physical or psychological. The Mexicans suffered the abuse, but because of their extreme spiritual strength, they have survived like the delicate butterfly or hummingbird or like the repugnant insects of the earth.

Mexicans adapted to their environment, Mexico City, the Golgotha of pollution, growing worse after the great ecological disasters. The Mexicans who lived there had no choice but to stay and cope. They were trapped in a historical and geographical bowl. Escape was impossible. The roads leading out of the capital were overrun by the masses entering the capital. Today, two individual roads, or causeways, north-south and east-west west, lead out of the capital. Strangely, these were the original causeways, the same routes used by the Aztecs when they ruled the valley of Tenochtitlan.

The text in Grandfather Gregory's library taught that, in the time of the Aztecs and in his time, scientist were heroes. Now, no scientific heroes were allowed to exist. We were all caught in the asymptote of knowledge, never quite touching the perfection humanity pursued.

The Triple Alliance Directorate maintained that apparatuses like Gabi's computer arm would bridge the infinite and minute space between us and perfection. The damage brought about by our efforts was only tests and obstacles put before us by the unknown wanting to be known. My discovery of an unknown was announced not by the Triple Alliance Directorate, but by Mr. and Mrs. Norton, who, along with their daughter, were immediately sequestered to an unknown location. All information concerning my discovery was suppressed by the Directorate and I was ordered to remain in my home in the exclusive Oakridge Ranches in the Higher Life Existence City of Temecula, California.

It had been three months since my detention. I had not been denied access to information from the outside. Gabi took over my position as director of the LAMEX Health Corridor and visited me every week, without fail. Gabi—my carnal link to the outside world.

The smell of burnt flesh reached me in the library as I continued reading from the written texts. I resisted the interruption. She had visited yesterday, and I did not expect her to return until the following week. The odor lingered and grew stronger. I heard her grumble while she began to recharge her arm. A light outlined her high cheekbones, finely sculptured lips and deep oval Asian eyes. The evening lights of Hemet glittered below in the clear autumn sky. I opened the window. The cool breeze beckoned. Not a word, as I felt her tenseness. . . . Not good news, I thought, as she reengaged that awesome appendage.

"They have forgiven you and dropped charges of withholding knowledge considered to be the Triple Alliance patrimony," Gabi said solemnly. "You're almost free."

The smell of charred human flesh persisted.

Gabi broke the hush. "Pack your bag. I've been ordered to take you to Los Angeles."

"What for?"

"Los Angeles has been hit by a major plague. We believe it came from the sea, through the harbor and into the shore. It has tentacles which penetrate the earth. It has not moved for a week. Thousands have died. Their lungs destroyed. I can't solve it. The Directorate wants you to try your experiments. I believe that you are our only chance."

"Who is dying? Gabi, who is dying?" I asked with a bitter taste in my mouth.

"Most of the casualties are Euroanglo and Japanese. I checked. Only those Mexicans born in this country have died. Not one from Mexico City. In fact, they are the ones who are helping in the hospitals. The Directorate has called in a military legion from Mexico City. You are to arrive at the same time," Gabi looked out over the valley.

"Why don't they do it? They know what they have to do."

"They simply don't want to. The majority of members of the Directorate have not yet overcome psychologically structured prejudices. Besides, you are the only one who has performed the transfusions. Damn it, Gregory! This is no time to question why." Gabi screamed. "People are dying. They need you to help them!"

She moved away from the window. She was crying. I wondered if it was for the dying or for her own failure to solve the disease.

"Gregory, it's horrible out there," Gabi sobbed. She did not restrain her emotions. My eyes welled up with tears. I recalled the feelings described in Grandfather Gregory's books. Human emotions, assumed trained and hypnotized out of us, now rushed in and overpowered our hearts. At that moment, I thought my heart would burst.

"When do we have to be there?" I asked.

"Tomorrow morning the legion is scheduled to arrive."

That night, Gabi fell into a deep sleep. The lights of her arm, like the sound of a leaking faucet, unsettled my sleep. Throughout the night I listened to her moans and incoherent talk as I waited for the sun to rise. At daybreak the image of the smiling Mexican soldier rose with the sun.

I wondered if I would see him again.

14

For days I worked in the outer ring of the city, cordoned off by the Triple Alliance soldiers. There, in the outer parameters of the plague-infested megalopolis, the workers who had escaped initial contamination huddled against the military barricades. Those who attempted to escape the quarantine never got as far as the distance of a shout before they were stopped or instantly obliterated. Here on the border, fewer people died. It seemed as if few were infected and those who died had come from the center of the quarantine area.

Thousands had perished and thousands more showed the symptoms of the plague. The initial infecting gases had evaporated or returned to the earth and probably to the sea, where from its mother's wet warmth it nourished and gathered more vigor, to strike again.

This human-made beast killed rapidly. First the victim complained of dizziness and fatigue, which intensified hourly, accompanied by difficulty in breathing. Finally, in the last hours, the blood vessels in the lungs became engorged, expanding the chest and back, eventually bursting, slowly rushing blood to the surface skin, causing a bluish red stain around the victim's upper torso. Victims died of a crushed heart or ruptured lungs. They drowned in their blood.

The disease came to full term within three to four days, depending on the strength of the person. Most victims died within two days, seemingly giving up life once they were told they had contracted Blue Buster, the name coined by the medical team first on the scene.

At night, I worked in the heart of the dying, at the center of the city, where Blue Buster killed the fastest. There were times I left the underground treatment centers and surfaced on to the streets. I watched the dead carried by family or friends to the cremation vehicles. Hadn't I seen this before, I thought. The massive tractors moved away tediously, stopping for the cries of late-comers. The bluish red ooze of blood had stained the city and the heavy odor of the abandoned dead buzzed in the polluted air.

This plague was beyond my experience. But I had read similar descriptions of it in Grandfather Gregory's books. With that thought, I turned a corner and there before me, standing in the putrid ooze of death were Grandfather Gregory and Papá Damián. They wrote what they had observed. Grandfather Gregory smiled and waved. He pointed to a group of three Triple Alliance soldiers that approached. They were members of the Mexico City division which had arrived with me. Papá Damián pointed to the soldier in the center. I watched as they passed. The young man in the middle was the Mexico City soldier whom I had met in San Diego. He smiled and kept walking with his companions. I turned to Grandfather Gregory and Papá Damián to thank them, but they kept on recording and did not acknowledge my presence. By the time I decided to speak to the Mexican soldier with the wonderful smile, he had disappeared into the suffering crowd of people.

Finally, after five days and after thousands of casualties, Gabi indicated that the Directorate had given their unconditional approval for the beginning of my experiments. It was obvious that the Directorate had a difficult time convincing the officers in command of the Mexico City legion that they should cooperate with the matter of blood donations. It was obvious that these warriors had a dual purpose. Here, they were the Triple Alliance military force in charge of the quarantine, and they were my official blood supply.

The decision as to who would participate in the transfusions had been made by Gabi and the Directorate. Patients who had been identified as contaminated with Blue Buster before twelve midnight were denied treatment and simply were condemned to die. Patients identified as suffering the initial symptoms after the time indicated were eligible for a blood transfusion. I understood that we could save only as many patients as we had Mexican soldiers. But even then, not all would survive. The others, we would tend to their pain. After they died, we would fling them into the abyss or the great dust whirlwinds of space. Gabi explained these conditions as she escorted me to where we would conduct the transfusions. I began immediately. By four that morning, I had supervised approximately one thousand transfusions. By dawn, people showed marked improvement.

Gabi had assisted me and learned the procedure, and the gender requirements. By the time the second thousand patients began the procedure, she knew everything I knew. Bleed the patient and transfuse genetically antidotal Mexican blood. It was amazingly primitive medicine.

At midday, a spirit of positive action, good-feeling and kindness overwhelmed the population at the center of the poisoned area. The rumors had become fact. The Mexican soldiers' blood had healing powers; it cured all lung disorders. Everyone concerned with the plague praised the spirit of volunteerism, the willingness of the soldiers to give blood to help the afflicted. The Mexican warriors were hailed as heroes. From mouth to mouth the news advanced swiftly through the streets, where the masses forsakened to the pestilence heard of the possibility of life. Their attention first turned to the entrance of the underground treatment centers, where they were refused an audience with the director of the LAMEX medical corridor. An atrocious hysteria overcame the crowds requesting treatment that had been refused to them days before. In less than an hour, absolute pandemonium engulfed Los Angeles. The lifesaving legion from Mexico City was ordered to fire on the unhealthy people. I caught a glimpse of the slaughter that rained in the streets as Gabi and I were whisked to an unknown destination.

Things began to fall apart. I no longer felt comfortable with Gabi, nor with what I was doing. I sensed eyes constantly observing me from the moment Gabi had arrived in my home. This sensation of heavy eyes was strongest minutes before Gabi ordered me to board a giant Triple Alliance copter. As the immense machine rose high over the city of Los Angeles, I feared that I forever might be in the custody of the Triple Alliance.

"The plague is under control," Gabi said. "And you did it!"

Proudly, Gabi made a fist with her computerized hand.

I watched Los Angeles disappear in the density of great smoke clouds ascending from the bluish-red hue of death below.

A great surge of power gently pushed me into my seat and in a matter of seconds the copter broke into an immense clear sky where I counted stunning bright stars. We soon descended into a green landing circle surrounded by a multitude of colorful flowers.

15

The view from here, high above the city of Los Angeles, was spectacular. Gabi and I walked through an expertly manicured herb garden which I imagined contained every herb in existence. The fortress was built into the side of a mountain and the only access was by helicopter. Beyond the gardens and patios there was open space, hundreds of feet direct to jagged hills below. As I followed Gabi through several corridors and rooms, I noted walls with thousands of books, the old books as in my grandfather's library. Finally Gabi turned into a large room with beautiful wooden balconies about twenty feet high around its walls. Above the balconies more volumes were stored. I could see several doors that led to other rooms filled with books. The house was a huge depository of knowledge stored in the old manner, in ancient beautiful books.

This must be the place where the Directorate has condemned me to live for the rest of my life, I thought. Of course, this is to be my prison, this cloister of paper books. How thoughtful of Gabi to have suggested that I be confined with one of my passions. I reached for one of the volumes.

"Just don't let her catch you reading that garbage or she'll throw us both out," Gabi interrupted my concentration.

Although I wanted to read the old text, for the moment I followed her advice and placed the book on a table where Grandfather Gregory and Papá Damián wrote down my every thought. Music from an adjoining room broke the silence. Three children, one boy and two girls, played a delightful, gay tune. One child played the piano, the other the violin, and the third the flute. Gabi and I listened for some time. The music filled my heart with peace and for

fifteen minutes the world did not exist. Only the wonderful sound of
harmony caressing my mind. Suddenly, the children stopped and
stood at attention.

What stopped them from playing this wonderful music was a
slender, dark woman who entered the room from a side door. With
a curious wag of her finger she dismissed the children and went
to Gabi, who shook her hand and exchanged a few words. Gabi
reached out toward me. The woman's deep set dark eyes scrutinized my approach. Her distinctly carved lips pursed tenderly, as
if inviting a kiss. The cut of her nose was slightly wide and elegant.
She wore her thick black hair back in a bun, exposing a jagged hair
line.

"Madam First Directorate, this is Doctor Gregory Revueltas,"
Gabi said and reached out for me to come closer.

She offered her hand. "So, you're the doctor with the funny
Mexican blood. I am Elena Tarn, First Directorate of the Triple
Alliance. I am pleased that you accepted my invitation to stay here
for a few days. I am sure that you will help me." Elena Tarn spoke
and walked to the table where I had left the book.

I responded without thinking. "I will do everything in my power
to meet your expectations, Madam First Directorate." Don Antonio
Pérez, the Man-god, came to mind, but his image would not suffice
to describe the power this woman possessed. Two soldiers entered
and waited to be recognized. They handed her documents, which
she signed. They left immediately.

Elena Tarn picked up the book I had selected and returned it to
its place on the shelf. "I know every book in this fortress. Later, at
your leisure, you may read the rest of this volume," Elena said and
formed a pyramid with her hands. She raised them above her head
and spoke through the pyramid. "But now you most cure my only
child, my daughter, Udina. She is struck down with the plague. For
five days she has suffered. You and your funny Mexican blood are
her last chance."

Elena Tarn smiled. Dimples formed on her cheeks. With Gabi

a step behind, I followed the First Directorate to a laboratory equal to our research center in Los Angeles.

As we moved closer to the patient, I wondered what my fate would be if I failed. I was sure Udina's condition was grave. She had been battered by the disease for five days and most people had died in three or four. Why did it have to be me to do the obvious? The only logical reason was that now I was uncomplicatedly expendable. Grandfather Gregory and Papá Damián had disappeared. I searched for them at every electronic microscope or chemical test table. They refused to be found. Gabi moved ahead and stopped with Elena Tarn. They stepped apart. I walked between them to confront a pitiful sight.

Elena Tarn went to her daughter's side. "She is alive still."

Udina lay naked on a white moveable marble slab in the center of the laboratory. Most life sustaining mechanisms that I knew were next to her. Some were attached. Others waited their desperate turn. Blood had risen and perforated the child's upper torso. The bluish-red stain covered most of her body. A yellowish mucosa streamed from several openings in the skin, which floated on a blood-like gel.

Udina's eyes opened slowly. She stared at her mother. Two assistants appeared and escorted us to a sterile operating room. We prepared while the patient was brought before me.

"You can begin the transfusion now," Elena Tarn ordered.

"And the blood?" I asked breathing slowly the fetid smell of Udina's decomposing flesh.

"The blood will be drawn from live specimens," Gabi explained and indicated to the assistants to bring forth the young Mexican male. The young man was brought on a white marble slab. I observed his fearful countenance and, to my great surprise, there lying naked and shivering before me was the smiling Mexican soldier of the Mexico City legion whom I had met in San Diego.

The Mexican soldier, who worshiped the sun and whose blood had started me on this journey, amicably offered his arm.

16

Gabi grabbed the manuscript from me, and holding it defiantly said, "Udina wants you to check her bandages!"

I walked away satisfied that I had spent practically the entire morning reading from the old books gathered in this fortress of forgotten knowledge. For a week, at my leisure, I studied the books and found beautifully written treasures.

I discovered a section in the archives which held literary documents and on a hunch I searched out and located a copy of Grandfather Gregory's manuscript entitled *The Rag Doll Plagues*. I was overjoyed. On my third reading of the novel, I felt that he had written about me.

I heard music as I neared Udina's private quarters, where two medical assistants prepared the child's bandages. By the third day after the transfusion, she breathed without the aid of any life support system. Her body was transfigured from decaying to living matter. However, Blue Buster did cause scarring and damage to her breasts. In a year, a good plastic surgeon would restore the epidermis to normal shape and color.

After scraping Udina's torso, we wrapped light bandages over the more severe scabs.

She wanted freedom of movement and insisted on less wrapping. I placed the last plastic tab on the sterile gauze and made my way back to the part of the library where Gabi found me. I entered an unfamiliar room and discovered two people looking out over the gardens. It was the smiling Mexican soldier and a young woman.

"*Buenas tardes, doctor,*" he said softly.

"*Para siempre,*" the young woman cried.

"*Para siempre*, forever," I repeated and walked out disgusted at the fate forced on them. They would live in privileged enslavement for the remainder of their lives. Their blood was worth lives and Elena Tarn guaranteed herself and her daughter an indefinite supply.

She wanted these Mexicans to produce children, for they inherited their parent's blood chemical qualities. The smiling Mexican soldier and the Mexican woman existed like expensive pets, producing excellent pedigree.

I left them in their reminiscence of home and found my way back to the library room where I had been all morning. There Elena Tarn discussed the future of the smiling Mexican soldier with Gabi.

"He chose to stay. As for the girl, I selected her myself from a group of Mexico City virgins. They can go anywhere they desire under the protection of my guards," Elena Tarn spoke irritably. She acknowledged my presence with a nod of her head.

"And as for you, Doctor Revueltas, you are to report back to the Los Angeles research center for further orders. Gabi will escort you there."

That was the last time I ever saw Elena Tarn.

Gabi adjusted her computer arm. The smell of singed flesh started to linger about her. I noticed her worried expression as she turned the arm tighter on to her elbow socket.

"Not another damn book," Gabi said. She was annoyed at the smell of her burning bone. "We leave in fifteen minutes," she barked while fidgeting with the arm's electrical connectors. As the copter descended onto the landing station at the Los Angeles research center, I thought that my stay with Elena and Udina Tarn had been for only a brief instant in time. I remembered Grandfather Gregory's novel and I was thankful that my stay here on earth would be just a little longer.

17

The population of people from Mexico City tripled in a matter of weeks. They came with their identification documents, birth certificates and letters of residence, certifying that they were born and had lived in Mexico City or in the surrounding area all their life. These people from ancient Tenochtitlan were in demand. They offered a mutated blood that was beneficial to people who had lived in the contaminated environment of Los Angeles and suffered gravely.

The Euroanglo population became the most aggressive in hiring and maintaining a Mexico City Mexican, an MCM, in residence. The Los Angeles folks offered a salary and room and board to guarantee their access to MCM blood. Many MCMs moved right in with the families and signed an agreement to offer their blood for sale. In months the MCM blood business soared to become a multimillion-dollar industry. Mexican blood was offered at reasonable prices to those that could not afford their own Mexican. The Triple Alliance prepared to produce it for the general public, but soon it became obvious that the Alliance's efforts could not keep up with the demand. Consequently, small production companies were established.

There came to exist blood farms. Mexicans were contracted and flown in from Mexico City to live in luxury and produce blood. Blood towns sprung up overnight. Large pharmaceutical companies purchased land on the outskirts of Los Angeles and constructed beautiful communities for the MCMs under contract to them. Some pharmaceuticals insisted on physical criteria: height, muscularity, facial looks, I.Q test and age. These companies admitted that they had breeder communities. They would contract single men and women who met their requirements and encouraged them to reproduce at their leisure and enjoyment. When the contract expired, they could choose someone to live with in a more legal relationship and take care of their children, or they could leave the children to the care of the company. The production of blood was of paramount importance. The self-reproduction of air pollutants was rising, not only in Los Angeles but in other long time industrial areas throughout the world. But the alarming frequency of lethal plagues that traveled from the sea, penetrated the earth and surfaced unpredictably to kill thousands was what motivated the production and storage of MCM blood.

The urgent need to possess Mexican blood reached the point of absurdity. The newspapers carried ridiculous articles about families fighting over one Mexican, or a family of Mexicans who refused to be separated. Euroanglos always wanted to be photographed with their Mexican at their side. People took their Mexicans everywhere, fearing that friends or relatives would steal them. Millions of MCMs signed contracts of blood enslavement. Here again, the Mexican population became the backbone of the LAMEX corridor.

In the past, it was Mexican Indian blood that was sacrificed to the sun forces; it was Mexican blood that was spilled during the conquest; it was Mexican blood that ran during the genocidal campaign of the Spanish Colonial period; it was Mexican blood that stained the bayonets during the war of Independence and the Mexican Revolution of 1910; it was Mexican blood that provided the cheap labor to California during the first half of the nineteenth century and that now provided the massive labor force in the *maquiladora* factory belt; it was Mexican blood that provided the millions of men and women that constituted more than ninety percent of the Triple Alliance military forces. It was Mexican blood that guaranteed a cure and prevention from lung disorders. In a matter of time Mexican blood would run in all the population of the LAMEX corridor. Mexican blood would gain control of the land it lost almost two hundred and fifty years ago.

This thought originated in Grandfather Gregory's long forgotten histories.

These were the conditions under which I worked for about one year, constantly monitored by Gabi and the Triple Alliance. My job was the collection and storage of MCM blood. I followed Gabi's directions and made no request out of the ordinary. I traveled daily from Temecula, California, to the Los Angeles research center. Gabi and I seldom visited and our feelings for each other faded away into our work. Gabi dedicated her life to the job she had always desired and she was doing quite well. For the moment, I was satisfied with the basic elements of my work and felt no compelling need to practice medicine. Vaguely familiar ideas, emotions and motivations broke into my thinking. I believe that these feelings had been repressed during my training and now they had surfaced, driving me to seek relationships that at one time I refused to cultivate. My life was exciting. I began to feel that I was capable of learning a new way of life, one in which basic human dignity was important. Ted and Amalia Chen offered this new vision of the world. I was thinking of them as the odor of seared flesh announced Gabi's presence.

She hurriedly entered the laboratory. Several people purposely changed direction to avoid her who, harried by the complications of her computerized arm, went immediately to an electrical charge unit. Gabi sat silently readying herself to connect her arm to the largest electrical conductor in the laboratory. A tired stare shadowed her countenance. Gabi's flesh had begun to reveal the damage of her life style, of the pressures of the job, of her arm that required more frequent recharging, and of the constant odor of an elbow that refused to heal and now probably had become a malignant infection. Her body rejected the synthetic adapters between the electronic arm and her human flesh and bone.

The computer arm experiment had been successful for the majority of those who had participated. Of the one hundred original participants, there were only a few rejections—Gabi Chung was one.

This knowledge devastated her desire for professional efficiency and perfection. The fact that she was not allowed to continue to the second stage of the medical robotics experiment unofficially announced her elimination from her present job. I knew that I was in her sight and I hoped she would call out to me, but instead she kept staring through me. Without further delay, she engaged her magic arm into the massive power circuit. Almost immediately the odor diminished. For a moment Gabi smiled as if she were being recharged with happiness.

I returned the smile and stepped toward her. At that instant, she reached for the voltage lever and raised it to the maximum capacity.

Without warning, before my eyes, my brilliant and once personal guide and assistant took into her body a voltage so great that her arms and legs popped open like spring rose buds, slowly exposing the inner color of their flower. Gabi's white blouse turned crimson as she fell backwards, leaving the mechanical appendage connected to the generator. Smoke smoldered from what was left of her flesh.

Several assistants cut the power. Others rushed to her side, and were repelled by the heat. As I moved away from the chaos, I glimpsed Gabi's nonexistent face and heard a terrible scream before I ran out of an emergency exit.

In that horrifying instant, I believed that I would find Gabi outside; all I had to do was search for her.

18

Hours after Gabi's suicide, I found myself being transported to a cave located in the center of a great volcano. In this place I was shown two magnificent rainbows whose ends marked four new sources of water. I was also given, for reasons which even to this day I ignore, a head made of crystal and four icons which represented the Light, the Palm, the Olive and the Lily.

At dawn, I was accompanied by Ted and Amalia Chen and we ceremoniously entered El Mar de Villas. I did not understand the reason for the ceremonies. Amalia was seven months pregnant. I remembered Ted saying that the people were jubilant for the return of the man who had saved the life of their child Man-god.

19

It has been about three years since that day of losing a loved one and of gaining a whole people. I am now the first advisor to the Man-god of El Mar de Villas and the director of its political and paramilitary sectors of El Mar de Villas.

El Mar de Villas has developed into the largest and most powerful sector of the LAMEX corridor. The Euroanglo population has continued to diminish and grow old while the Mexican population keeps getting larger.

Recently, the Mexican warriors of the Triple Alliance forced the Directorate to substitute four of their members with Mexican representatives. One of the deposed members of the Directorate happened to be Elena Tarn. Don Antonio Pérez's son, the child Man-god of El Mar de Villas, to whom I have sworn allegiance and serve faithfully, was appointed to take her place. My official residence is Elena Tarn's fortress, which I call Library. This building and its contents were awarded to me for my loyal service to the field of science and humanity. These recognitions were given to me by the Man-god of El Mar de Villas. However, I prefer to live in a simple house in El Mar de Villas and periodically visit my home in Temecula.

The chaotic pursuit of Mexican blood subsided once the Blue Buster plague calmed. But even after its control, one could find at least two Mexico City Mexicans—a female and a male—in every family.

From up here, surrounded by thousands of books, I wonder when will I have time to love a woman and have children, like normal people did in the late twentieth century. I can only protect and enjoy Ted and Amalia's baby, for that child represents the hope for the new millennium.

I am no longer me. I am transfigured into all those that have gone before me: my progenitors, my hopeful ever-surviving race. From the deepest part of my being there rushes to the surface of my almond shaped eyes an ancient tear.

ACI 5433   3/31/92